"Lesley, listen to me," Chase whispered.

"No," she whispered back. She didn't want to talk. All she wanted was for Chase to hold her.

In his arms she could feel again. For months she'd been trapped—not dead, yet not alive, either, her emotions stretched so thin she felt nothing but numb. Then she'd met Chase, and suddenly she was laughing again, dreaming again, a kaleidoscope of feelings flooding her heart.

She didn't know what was happening to her, wasn't sure how to explain it or if she should even try. She didn't want to think. Because if she analyzed what she was doing *too* carefully, she might just change her mind.

So she simply wound her arms around his neck and hung on, hoping their white-hot passion would burn away her doubts....

MAIN

Dear Reader,

Welcome to Silhouette **Special Edition** . . . welcome to romance.

Last year, I requested that you send me your opinions on the books that we publish, and on romances in general. Thank you so much for the many thoughtful letters. For the next couple of months, I'd like to share some quotes from these letters with you. This seemed very appropriate now while we are in the midst of the THAT SPECIAL WOMAN! promotion. Each one of our readers is a special woman, as heroic as the heroines in our books.

This September has some wonderful stories coming your way. *A Husband to Remember* by Lisa Jackson is our THAT SPECIAL WOMAN! selection for this month.

This month also has other special treats. For one, we've got *Bride Wanted* by Debbie Macomber coming your way. This is the second book in her FROM THIS DAY FORWARD series. *Night Jasmine* by Erica Spindler—one of the BLOSSOMS OF THE SOUTH series—is also on its way to happy readers, as is Laurie Paige's *A Place for Eagles,* the second tale in her WILD RIVER TRILOGY. And September brings more books from favorite authors Patricia Coughlin and Natalie Bishop.

I hope you enjoy this book, and all of the stories to come!

Sincerely,

Tara Gavin
Senior Editor
Silhouette Books

Quote of the Month: "All the Silhouettes I've read have believable characters and are easy to identify with. The pace of the story line is good, the books hold my interest. When I start a Silhouette, I know I'm in for a good time."
                                                                —P. Digney,
                                                                New Jersey

Books by Debbie Macomber

Silhouette Special Edition

Starlight #128
Borrowed Dreams #241
Reflections of Yesterday #284
White Lace and Promises #322
All Things Considered #392
The Playboy and the Widow #482
°*Navy Wife* #494
°*Navy Blues* #518
For All My Tomorrows #530
Denim and Diamonds #570
Fallen Angel #577
*The Courtship of
   Carol Sommars* #606
†*The Cowboy's Lady* #626
†*The Sheriff Takes a Wife* #637
°*Navy Brat* #662
°*Navy Woman* #683
°*Navy Baby* #697
‡*Marriage of Inconvenience* #732
‡*Stand-in Wife* #744
‡*Bride on the Loose* #756
Hasty Wedding #798
+*Groom Wanted* #831
+*Bride Wanted* #836

°Navy Series
†The Manning Sisters
‡Those Manning Men Trilogy
+From This Day Forward
*Legendary Lovers Trilogy

Silhouette Romance

That Wintry Feeling #316
Promise Me Forever #341
Adam's Image #349
The Trouble with Caasi #379
A Friend or Two #392
Christmas Masquerade #405
Shadow Chasing #415
Yesterday's Hero #426
Laughter in the Rain #437
Jury of His Peers #449
Yesterday Once More #461
Friends—And Then Some #474
Sugar and Spice #494
No Competition #512
Love 'n' Marriage #522
Mail Order Bride #539
**Cindy and the Prince* #555
**Some Kind of Wonderful* #567
*Almost Paradise #579
Any Sunday #603
Almost an Angel #629
The Way to a Man's Heart #671

Silhouette Books

Silhouette Christmas Stories 1986
"Let It Snow"
to Mother with Love 1993
"The Apartment"

DEBBIE MACOMBER

hails from the state of Washington. As a busy wife and
mother of four, she strives to keep her family healthy
and happy. As the prolific author of dozens of best-
selling romance novels, she strives to keep her readers
happy with each new book she writes.

Dearest Friends,

I've always found a mail-order bride story to be one of the most romantic and wanted to include one in my latest trilogy. When I discovered romance novels, I dug through shelves of books looking for this type of plot. I was curious to learn what would prompt a woman to marry a virtual stranger and move away from everything that was familiar.

Chase Goodman, my hero in *Bride Wanted*, answered this question for me. He's exactly the kind of man who would persuade me to pack my bags and move to Alaska. Chase has decided he's lonely and he'd like to marry, but he only has a limited time to find himself a wife. Being a prudent man, he goes about obtaining one in the most practical way he can imagine. He advertises on a Seattle billboard.

The last thing Lesley Campbell is interested in at the moment is a husband. She's having enough trouble dealing with a broken engagement. As far as she's concerned, men are nothing but trouble. That's before she meets Chase and the fun begins.

I hope you enjoy this second installment in the FROM THIS DAY FORWARD trilogy. I love to hear from my readers and I'd love to know how you enjoyed this trilogy. You can write to me at:
P.O. Box 1458,
Port Orchard, WA 98366

Warmest wishes,

Debbie Macomber

Prologue

"Let me see if I've got this right," the man smoking the cigar behind the desk asked Chase Goodman. "You want to rent a billboard and advertise for a wife."

Chase wasn't about to let a potbellied cynic talk him out of the idea. He had exactly three weeks to find himself a bride and that didn't leave space for a lot of romantic nonsense. His time away from Alaska was limited and this was the most direct route he could think for getting himself a wife. He was thirty-three, relatively good-looking and lonesome as hell. He'd spent his last winter alone.

Okay, he was willing to admit, his idea was a tad unorthodox, but he was on a tight schedule. He intended to wine and dine the right woman, sweep her off her feet, but he figured he had to meet her first. Seattle was full of eligible women, but he wasn't fool enough to believe more than a few would be willing to leave the comforts of city life for the frozen north. The way Chase figured it, it was best to lay his cards on the table, wait and see what kind of response he got.

"You heard me right," Chase said stiffly.

"You want the billboard to read BRIDE WANTED?" The fat cigar moved as if by magic from one side of his mouth to the other.

"Yes, with the phone number I gave you. The answering service will be screening the calls."

"You considered what sort of women are going to be responding to that advertisement?"

Chase simply nodded. He had given a good deal of thought to exactly that question. He knew what to expect. But there was bound to be one who'd strike his fancy and if everything went as he'd like, he'd strike her fancy, too. That was what he was looking for, that shot in the dark, that one in a thousand.

He knew that it wasn't the best plan. If he had more time to woo a woman the way he wanted, he could prove that he intended to be a good husband, and God willing, a father when the time came. He wasn't like a lot of men with a smooth tongue who could blithely say the things a woman naturally wants to hear. He needed help and the billboard would set matters straight right from the first.

"I'll have my men on it first thing in the morning."

"Great," Chase said and grinned.

The wheels were now in motion. All he had to do was sit back and wait for his bride to come to him.

Chapter One

Lesley Campbell glared at the calendar accusingly. June fifteenth was to have been her wedding day. Only, she wasn't going to be a bride. The wedding dress hanging in the back of her closet would eventually yellow with age, unworn and neglected. Given Seattle's damp climate, the lovely silk-and-lace gown would probably mildew.

All right, Lesley decided, and with her natural flair for drama, she squared her shoulders. She was a better woman than to let a little thing like a broken engagement get her down. Her life was full. She had good friends—really good friends. Surely one of them would realize the significance of this day and call her. Jo Ann wouldn't forget this was to have been her wedding day and neither would Lori. Lesley couldn't ask for two better friends than her fellow teachers, Jo Ann and Lori. Both would have been her bridesmaids. They'd remember and were probably planning something special to console her. Something unexpected. A surprise. Something to chase away the blues and make her laugh.

The hollow feeling in the pit of her stomach seemed to yawn wider and Lesley flattened her hands against her abdomen. Closing her eyes, she breathed in deeply until the pressure lessened. She refused to give Tony the power to hurt her. It was bad enough that they continued to work together. Thank heaven, school had been dismissed for the summer the week before and she had three months to regroup and recuperate.

Lesley opened her refrigerator and looked inside, hoping something appetizing would magically appear. The same shriveled head of lettuce, two overripe tomatoes and a sick-looking zucchini stared back at her. It was just as well; she didn't have much of an appetite anyway.

Men—who needed them? Lesley mused as she closed the refrigerator door. Not her. Not ever again. She refused to become vulnerable to their fickle ways a second time.

Several of her friends had tested their matchmaking skills on her in the past several months, but Lesley's attitude was jaded. Whose wouldn't be?

The man she loved, the man she'd dedicated three years of her life to, had announced six months before their wedding that he needed more time. *More time.* Lesley had been incredulous. They'd dated the last two years of college, gone through the demands of student teaching together. They even worked at the same elementary school, saw each other on a daily basis and then, out of the blue, Tony had insisted he needed more time.

It wasn't until a week later that Lesley discovered *more time* meant he'd fallen head over heels in love with the first-grade teacher. Within three weeks of meeting April Packard, Tony had broken his engagement to Lesley. If that wasn't bad enough, Tony and April were married a month later, following a whirlwind courtship. Since she was under contract, and her savings slim, Lesley simply couldn't leave the school and she had been forced to endure the sight of the happy couple on a daily basis ever since.

She worked hard at not being bitter, at pretending it was all for the best. If Tony was going to fall in love with another woman, then it was better to have discovered this penchant of his before the wedding. She'd heard all the platitudes, tried to believe them, tried to console herself with them.

Only they didn't work.

She hurt. Some nights she wrestled with the loneliness until dawn; the feeling of abandonment nearly suffocated her. It didn't help matters to realize how happy Tony and April were.

He'd tried to make it up to Lesley. He'd looked to her to assuage his guilt. Because they worked in such close proximity, there was nothing she could do but repeat the platitudes others had given her. For the last month of school, she'd been forced to make believe a broken heart didn't matter.

Only, it did.

The last time she'd felt this empty inside had been as a six-year-old child, when her father had arranged for the family to fly to Disneyland. Lesley had been excited for weeks. It would have been her first trip in an airplane, her first time away from Washington State. Then three days before the vacation was to begin, her father had packed his bags and left the family, without warning, without a word of farewell to her, apparently without regret, taking the money they'd saved for the family trip.

Her mother was so trapped in her shock and grief that she hadn't been able to comfort Lesley, who'd been left feeling guilty and not knowing why.

As an adult she chose to forgive her father, and accept that he was a weak man, the same way she'd opted to absolve Tony for the pain he'd caused her. It would do no good to harbor a grudge or to feed her discontent.

Although it was easy to accept these facts on a conscious level, it took more than logic to convince her heart. Twenty years had passed since that fateful summer, but the feelings were as painful and as complex now as they had been to the little girl who dreadfully missed her daddy.

When neither Jo Ann nor Lori had phoned her by noon, Lesley's mood sank ever lower. It made sense that neither of them would call her, she reasoned. They might be thinking she'd forgotten what day it was. It wouldn't be worth dragging the whole ugly affair through the mud. All Lesley wanted to do was something fun, something that would make her forget how isolated she felt.

Jo Ann wasn't home, so Lesley left an upbeat message on her answering machine. The significance of the day seemed to have slipped past Lori, as well, who was all starry-eyed these days over a man she'd recently started dating.

"Any chance you can get away for a movie tonight?" Lesley asked.

Lori hemmed. "Not tonight. Larry's been out of town for the last couple of days and he'll be back this evening. He said something about dinner. Can we make it later in the week?"

"Sure," Lesley said, as though she hadn't a care in the world. Far be it for her to remind one of her two best friends that she was suffering the agonies of the jilted. "Have fun."

Some telltale inflection must have caught in her voice because Lori picked up on it immediately. "Lesley, are you all right?"

"Of course." It was always *of course*. Always something flippant that discounted her distress. "We'll get together later in the week."

They chatted for a few minutes longer. When they finished, Lesley knew it was up to her to make the best of this day. She couldn't rely on her friends, nor should she.

She mused over the realization for several moments, trying to decide what she was going to do. Attending a movie alone held no appeal nor did treating herself to dinner in a fancy restaurant. She sighed and bit into her lower lip, swallowing down the pain as she had so often before. She was sick of pretending it didn't hurt, tired to death of being cheerful and glib when her heart was breaking.

A day such as this called for drastic measures. Nothing got more drastic than a quart of chocolate-chip cookie-dough ice cream and a rented movie.

Lesley's spirits soared. It was perfect. Drowning her sorrows in decadence made up for a multitude of pretended indifferences. Men! Who needed them? Not her, Lesley decided. Not her.

She reached for her purse and was out the door filled with intention. Already her heart felt lighter.

It was while she was at a stoplight that Lesley first saw the billboard. BRIDE WANTED. PHONE 555-1213. At first she was amused. A man advertising for a bride? She'd never heard anything so ridiculous in her life. The guy was either a lunatic or a moron. Probably both. Then again, she reasoned, she wasn't exactly sympathetic to the male species lately. She'd been done wrong and she wasn't going to sweetly smile and forget it! Those days were long behind her.

Still mildly amused by the billboard, Lesley parked her car in the grocery store parking lot and headed toward the entrance. Colorful bedding plants, small rosebushes, and rhododendrons were sold in the front of the store, and she toyed with the idea of buying a few red geraniums and potting them in the porch planter box.

She noticed the man pacing the front of the automatic glass doors almost immediately. He seemed agitated and impatient, glancing at his watch every few seconds. Thinking nothing more of the matter, she focused her attention on the hanging baskets of bright pink fuchsias, musing how nice they'd look on her front porch.

"Excuse me," the man said when she approached. "Would you happen to have the time?"

"Sure," she said, raising her arm to glance at her wrist.

Without warning, the man reached for her purse, jerking it from her forearm so fast that for a moment Lesley stood frozen with shock and disbelief. She'd just been mugged. By the time she recovered, he'd sprinted halfway across the lot.

"Help! Thief!" she screamed as loud as she could. Knowing better than to wait for someone to rescue her, she took off at a dead run after the mugger, determined not to become his latest victim.

He was fast, she'd say that for him, but Lesley hadn't danced her way through all those aerobic classes for nothing. She may not be an Olympic hopeful, but she could hold her own.

The mugger was almost to the street, ready to vault around the corner, when another man flew past her. She didn't get a good look at him, other than that he was big and tall and wore a plaid shirt and blue jeans.

"He's got my purse," she shouted after him. Knowing she'd never catch the perpetrator herself, her only chance was the second man. She slowed to a trot in an effort to catch her breath.

To her relief, the second man chased after the thief and tackled him to the ground. Lesley's heart leapt to her throat as the pair rolled and briefly struggled. She reached them a few moments later not knowing what to expect. Her rescuer was holding the thief to the ground with his superior size and strength. Lesley watched as he easily retrieved her purse.

"I believe this belongs to you," her rescuer said, handing her the handbag.

The mugger kicked for all his worth, which in Lesley's eyes wasn't much. He was cursing, too, and doing a far more effective job of that.

"That's no way to talk in front of a lady," her hero stated calmly, turning the thief onto his stomach and pressing his knee into the middle of the mugger's back. The man on the ground groaned and shut up.

A police siren blared in the background.

"Who called the police?" Lesley asked, looking around until she saw a businessman holding on to a cellular phone. "Thanks," she shouted and waved.

The black-and-white patrol car pulled into the parking lot and eased to a stop. The patrolman stepped out of the car.

"Can either of you tell me what's going on here?" he asked.

"That man," Lesley said indignantly, pointing to the one sprawled on the asphalt, "grabbed my purse and took off running. And that man," she said, pointing to the one who'd run down the first, "caught him."

"Chase Goodman," her white knight said. He kept his foot pressed against the small of the thief's back as he nodded formally.

Lesley clenched her handbag to her breast, astonished at how close she'd come to losing everything. Her car keys were in her purse, along with her identification, checkbook, money and credit cards. Had she lost all her identification, it would have been a nightmare to replace everything. Nor would she have felt safe knowing someone had the keys to her home and her car, along with her address. The thought chilled her to the bone.

It seemed there were a hundred questions that needed answering before the police escorted the mugger to the station.

"I'm very grateful," Lesley said, studying the man who'd rescued her purse. He was tall—well over six feet—and big. It surprised her that anyone as massive could move with such speed. At first glance she guessed he was a bodybuilder, his upper torso was thick and well proportioned, but on closer inspection she decided he wasn't the type who spent his time in a gym. He had a rugged, outdoors look about him that Lesley found strongly appealing. A big, gentle, "bear" of a man. A gym would have felt confining to a man like Chase. Adding to his attraction were a pair of deep, dark brown eyes and a friendly smile.

"My pleasure, Miss..."

"Lesley Campbell. How'd you know I wasn't married?"

"No ring."

Her thumb absently moved over the groove in her finger where Tony's engagement ring had once been and she nodded. He wasn't wearing one, either.

"Do you do this sort of thing for a living?"

"Excuse me?" Chase smiled at her, looking a bit confused.

"Run after crooks, I mean," Lesley explained. "Are you an off-duty policeman or something?"

"No, I work on the Alaskan pipeline. I'm visiting Seattle for the next few weeks."

"That explains it," she said absently.

"Explains what?"

She hadn't realized he'd heard her. "What I was thinking about you. That you're an open-air kind of person." It mildly surprised her that she'd read him so well. Generally she wasn't as perceptive.

Her insight appeared to please him because he smiled once more. "Would you like to know what I was thinking about you?"

"Sure." She probably shouldn't be so curious, but it wouldn't do any harm.

"You run like a gazelle, with agility and grace, and that you're the first woman I've met in a long while who doesn't have to throw back her head to look up at me."

"That's true enough." Lesley understood what it meant to be tall. She was five-eleven herself and had been the tallest girl in her high school class. Her height had been a curse and in some ways her greatest asset. As a youngster, her teachers assumed that because she was taller she should be more mature, smarter, a leader, and so she'd been burdened with those expectations. Buying clothes had always been a problem, along with attracting boys. It was only when she entered her twenties that she decided to be proud of who and what she was. Once she refused to apologize for her size, she seemed to attract the opposite sex. It was shortly after that when she'd met Tony. It had never bothered her that he was an inch shorter than she, nor had it seemed to trouble him.

They were walking back toward the grocery store. "You're a runner?"

"Heavens no," Lesley answered, complimented by the assumption.

They were standing under the hanging fuchsia baskets when Lesley realized they had no reason to continue their discussion. "I'd like to thank you for your help," she said, opening her purse and taking out her wallet.

He placed his hand on hers, his touch gentle but insistent. "I won't take your money."

"I'd never have caught him without you. It's the least I can do."

"I did what anyone would have done."

"Hardly," Lesley countered. The lot had been full of people and no one else had chased the mugger. No one else had been willing to become involved. She'd received plenty of sympathetic looks, but no one other than Chase had been willing to help her.

"If you insist upon thanking me, then how about a cup of coffee?"

Lesley's gaze went to the café, situated next to the grocery store in the strip mall. She'd just been mugged and having coffee with a stranger didn't seem to be an especially brilliant idea.

"I can understand your hesitation, but I assure you I'm harmless."

"All right," Lesley found herself agreeing. Chase smiled and his brown eyes fairly sparkled. She'd rarely known a man with more expressive eyes.

They took a table by the window and the waitress delivered plastic-coated menus and listed the specials of the day.

"I'll just have coffee," Lesley said.

"What kind of pie do you have?" Chase wanted to know.

The waitress, a teenager with a complexion problem, listed five varieties in a monotone voice as if she said the same words no less than five hundred times a day.

"Give me a piece of the apple pie and a cup of coffee."

"I'll take a slice of that pie, too," Lesley said. "I shouldn't," she muttered to Chase when the waitress left, "but I'm going to indulge myself." She'd forgo the gourmet ice cream and drown her blues in an old Doris Day movie, where love seemed to work out right and everything fell neatly into place just before THE END rolled onto the screen. If ever there was a time she needed to believe in fairy tales, it was this day.

"Sure you should," Chase said.

"I know," Lesley said, straightening and looking out the window as she remembered the reason she was pampering herself. It embarrassed her acutely when tears flooded her eyes. She managed to blink them back but not before Chase noticed.

"Is something wrong?"

"Delayed shock, I guess," she said, hoping that sounded logical, and that he'd accept it without further inquiry. Funny, she could go weeks without dwelling on the pain and then the minute school was out and Tony and April weren't around, she started weeping.

"It's just that today was supposed to have been my wedding day," she blurted out. For the life of her, Les-

ley didn't know what caused her to announce this humiliation to a complete stranger.

"What happened?" Chase asked softly. His hand
reached for her, his fingers folding around hers in a
comforting, reassuring way.

"Oh, what usually happens in these instances. Tony
met someone else and . . . well, I guess it was just one of
those things. The two of them clicked, and after a whirlwind courtship, they were married. They both seem
happy. It's just that . . ." Her voice faltered and she left
the rest unsaid.

The waitress delivered the pie and coffee and, grateful
for the intrusion, Lesley reached for her purse and took
out a tissue. "My friends forgot that today was the day
Tony and I'd originally set for the wedding. In retro-
spect, I don't know if I miss him as much as I miss having the big fancy wedding. I had everything planned,
right down to the type of flowers we would use for the
pew bows. It was going to be a perfect day.

"I guess I became so involved in getting ready for the
wedding that I didn't notice how unhappy and restless
Tony had become. When he asked for time to think everything through, I was shocked. I should have realized
then that something was troubling him. As it turned out,
it was good old-fashioned guilt. He'd met April. . . . We
all work at the same elementary school."

"Teachers?"

Lesley nodded. "Anyway, he was attracted to April,
and she to him, and the whole thing got out of control. . . . I'm sure you get the picture."

"Yes, I do. It seems to me that your friend is a fool."

Lesley laughed and it sounded more like a hiccup than
any real amusement. "We're still friends, or at least he
tries to be my friend. I don't know what I feel—not any-

more. It all happened months ago, but it still hurts and I can't seem to put it behind me.''

"It's only human that you should feel betrayed and hurt, especially today.''

"Yes, I know, but it's much more than that. Tony felt terrible about the whole thing and with all of us working together, well that just makes it more difficult. I asked the school district for a transfer but when Tony heard about it, he came to me. He feels so damn guilty.''

"As well he should.''

"I know it was a mistake, but I withdrew the request.'' Lesley didn't know what had prompted her to rehash the details of her broken engagement, especially with a stranger. It felt better to speak of it somehow, to relieve her mind with the weight of her unhappiness.

Lesley lowered her gaze and took a deep breath. "Listen, I'm sorry to burden you with this,'' she said in a calmer tone.

"No, you needed to talk and I'm honored that you told me. I mean that. Have you been seeing anyone else since?''

"No.'' Lesley sliced into her pie with the side of her fork. "Lately I find myself feeling cynical about relationships. I'm almost convinced love, marriage and all that simply aren't worth the effort...although I would like to have children someday,'' she added thoughtfully.

"Cynical, huh? Does that mean you don't date at all? Not *ever?*''

"I don't date and don't intend to for a long while. I'm not sympathetic toward men, either. On the way to the store just now, I saw the most ridiculous billboard. Some guy claimed he was looking for a bride and listed his phone number, and instead of feeling sorry for the guy, I laughed.''

"Sorry for the guy?" Chase asked. He'd already finished his pie and was cupping the ceramic mug of coffee with both hands.

"Think about it. What kind of man advertises for a wife? One who's old and ugly and desperate, right?"

"What makes you say that?"

"If he can't find a wife any other way, there must be something wrong with him. If that isn't cause for sympathy I don't know what is."

"You think the women who respond will be old and ugly, as well?" Chase asked, frowning.

"Heavens, I wouldn't know. I don't understand men. I've tried, but I seem to be missing something. Tony was the only man I ever considered marrying and...well, I've already told you what happened to that relationship."

"In other words, you'd never think of dating a man who advertised for a wife?" Chase asked.

"Never," she assured him emphatically. "But my guess is that he'll get plenty of takers."

"The old coot's probably lonely and looking for a little feminine companionship," Chase supplied.

"Exactly," she agreed, smiling softly as she mentally envisioned the man who was so desperate to advertise for a wife. "One would think I'd feel a little empathy for the guy, but I didn't. Instead I was amused."

"You think other women will laugh, too?"

Lesley shrugged. "I don't know, perhaps." Women like herself, maybe. The jaded and emotionally crippled ones.

"How long will you be in town?" she asked in an effort to divert the conversation away from herself. Nor was she eager to reveal how demented her thinking had become.

"Another two and a half weeks. I can't take city living much longer than that. The noise gets to me."

"You've been in Seattle before?"

"I come every year about this time. I generally visit the Pacific Northwest but am partial to San Francisco, too. By the end of my vacation I'm more than ready to return to the tundra."

"I've heard Alaska is very beautiful," Lesley said conversationally.

"There's a peace there, an untouched beauty that never fails to reach me. I've lived there all my life and still it fascinates me, still it touches my soul."

Lesley was mesmerized by his words and the serenity she sensed in him. How badly she needed that for herself. "What city are you from?"

"It's a little town in the northern section of the state called Twin Creeks. I doubt that you've heard of it. I won't kid you. The winters are cold and harsh, and there isn't a lot to do for entertainment. By mid-December the amount of light is counted in minutes, not hours. By contrast, the sun's out past midnight this time of the year."

"Other than your job, what do you do to occupy yourself in the dead of winter?" It fascinated her that someone would actually choose to live in such a harsh environment.

"Read and study mostly. I do a bit of writing now and again."

"It sounds peaceful."

"It is," he assured her. "Often too peaceful."

They'd both finished their pie and coffee and the waitress returned with the pot for refills. Lesley didn't understand his comment, and let it pass. This was probably the reason he came to Seattle every year, to kick up his heels and party. Yet he didn't look like the party animal. His idea of the wild life was probably drinking beer in a hot tub, Lesley thought, smiling to herself.

"Something amuses you?"

Lesley instantly felt guilty. She was becoming more condescending than she realized. Chase was a gentleman, a gentle giant who had kindly stepped in to help her when all those around her had chosen to ignore her plight. Remorse burdened her heart.

"Thank you again," Lesley said, reaching for the tab.

"No," Chase whispered, removing the slip from her fingers, "thank you for the pleasure of your company."

"Please, picking up the cost of the pie and coffee is such a little thing to do to thank you for your help. Don't deny me that."

He hesitated and then nodded, giving it back to her. "With one condition."

Lesley walked over to the cash register and paid the tab before Chase changed his mind, before he could set his conditions.

"What's that?" she asked, slipping the change into her coin purse.

"That you have dinner with me."

Her first inclination was to refuse. She wasn't interested in dating and hadn't in months. She had told him as much very plainly. She wasn't ready to become involved in a relationship, not even with a man who was a tourist and who'd be out of her life in a few weeks. Besides, he was a stranger. Other than his name and a few other pertinent details, what did she know about him?

He must have read the doubts in her eyes.

"You choose the time and the place and I'll meet you there," he suggested. "You're wise to be cautious."

Still she hesitated.

"I promise I won't disappoint you the way Todd did."

"Tony," she corrected. It amused and frustrated her how quickly she found herself wanting to defend Tony, wanting to discount what he'd done to her.

"One dinner," Chase added. "That's all I ask."

Lesley sighed, feeling herself weakening. If she refused, she'd be stuck watching Doris Day and Rock Hudson and eating ice cream in her sweats in front of the television. The image wasn't a pretty one.

"All right," she found herself saying, with a decisiveness she didn't feel. "Six o'clock, at Salty's at Rodondo."

"I'll make reservations."

"No," she said quickly. "I've changed my mind.... Don't make it Salty's." That had been her and Tony's restaurant. "Let's try the Seattle waterfront. I'll meet you in front of the aquarium at six and we can find someplace to eat around there."

His smile touched his eyes and he nodded. "I'll be there."

Chapter Two

Chase Goodman stepped from the shower and reached for the thick hotel towel. He'd turned on the television and was standing in the bathroom doorway listening to snippets of news while he dried his hair.

He dressed in slacks and a crisp blue shirt, hoping Lesley didn't expect him to wear a tie. Gray slacks and a decent dress shirt was as good as he got. A regular tie felt like a hangman's noose and he'd look damn silly in a bow tie. Generally he didn't worry about what a woman thought, but he liked Lesley.

That was the problem. He liked her, really liked her. The hollow feeling hadn't left his stomach from the moment they'd parted. It was the kind of sensation a man gets when he knows something's about to happen, something profound. Something good. It felt like an emotional kick in the butt.

He liked that she was tall and not the least bit apologetic about it. Petite women were nice, but he preferred a woman he didn't have to worry about hurting every time he held her. His size intimidated a lot of women, but not Lesley. She had grit, real grit. It wasn't every woman who'd race after a mugger.

Lesley wasn't stunningly beautiful nor did she have perfect features. Her face was a little too square, and her hair a dusty shade of blond. Not quite brown and not quite fair, but caught somewhere in between. It reminded him of the color of the midnight sun at dusk.

Her eyes attracted him, too. He couldn't remember a darker shade of brown, almost as dark as his own, which were nearly the color of mahogany.

Chase was physically attracted to Lesley and the strength of that fascination took him by surprise. It confused and unsettled him. He'd come to Seattle to find himself a wife, had gone about it in a direct and straightforward manner. It didn't get much more direct than to take out a billboard advertisement.

He wanted to develop his relationship with Lesley, but he was worried. Lesley was vulnerable and hurting just now. If he concentrated his efforts on her, romanced her, even convinced her to marry him, he'd never be certain he hadn't taken advantage of her and her battered heart. Even worse, she might feel he had. Even knowing this did nothing to dampen his eager anticipation of their evening together. One night. That was all he wanted. One night and then he'd be better able to judge. One night and afterward he could decide what he was going to do, if anything.

Sitting on the edge of the mattress, Chase reached for the TV controller and turned up the volume, hoping the newscaster would take his mind off the feisty woman who attracted him so strongly. Not that it was likely. He hadn't felt that swift emotional kick for nothing.

"Hi ya, doll," Daisy said, letting herself into Lesley's front door after a couple of hard knocks. "I'm not interrupting anything, am I?"

"Sit down," Lesley said, aiming an earring toward her left ear and having troubling locating the hole without the help of a mirror. "Do you want some ice tea?"

"Sure, but I'll get it." Lesley watched as her neighbor walked into the kitchen and helped herself to two tall glasses from the cupboard. She poured two glasses from the pitcher in the refrigerator. "I'm glad to see you're going out," Daisy said, handing Lesley one of them. "I don't think it's a good idea for you to spend this evening alone."

It warmed Lesley's heart that someone had remembered the significance of this day. "The date slipped by Jo Ann and Lori."

"So what are you doing? Taking yourself out to dinner?" Daisy was nothing if not direct. Her neighbor didn't have the time to waste being subtle. She attended computer classes during the day and worked weekends as a cocktail waitress. Lesley admired her friend for taking control of her life, for getting out of a rotten marriage and struggling to do what was right for her and her two boys.

Her neighbor was a little rough around the edges, a little too honest and a little too direct, but she was one hell of a friend. Besides school and a job, she was a good mother to Kevin and Eric. Daisy's mother watched the boys during the days now that school was out, but it wasn't an ideal situation. The boys, seven and eight, were a handful. A teenage girl from the neighborhood fulfilled the duties the nights Daisy worked.

"How does this dress look?" Lesley asked, ignoring Daisy's question about taking herself out to dinner. She twirled to give Daisy a look at the simple blue-and-white-patterned dress. The skirt flared out at the knees as she spun around.

"New?" Daisy asked, helping herself to a handful of grapes from the fruit bowl in the center of the table. She trapped a seedless red grape between her two-inch-long nails and popped it into her mouth.

"Relatively new," Lesley said and lowered her gaze. "I've got a date."

"A *real* date?"

"Yes, I met him this afternoon. I was mugged and Chase—that's his name—caught the thief for me."

"In other words, Chase chased him."

"Exactly." She smiled at the way Daisy had of turning a phrase.

"You sure you can trust this guy?"

Lesley took a moment to analyze what she knew about Chase Goodman. Her impression was of steel strength, hued by eyes that smiled with a gentle, fun-loving spirit. Physically he was six four, possibly taller, his chest was wide and his shoulders were thick. Despite his size, he ran with the grace of an athlete. Her overall impression of Chase was of total, unequivocal masculinity. The type of man who worked hard, lived hard and loved hard.

Her cheeks flushed with color at the thought of Chase in bed.

"I can trust him," Lesley answered. It was herself she needed to question. If she was still desperately in love with Tony, then she shouldn't be attracted to Chase, but she was. She barely knew the man, and yet she felt as if she were completely safe with him, completely at ease. She must, otherwise she wouldn't have blurted out the humiliating details of her broken engagement. She'd never done anything like that with anyone else.

"I'm meeting Chase at the Seattle aquarium at six," Lesley elaborated.

"He sounds like he just might be hero material," Daisy said, reaching for a small cluster of grapes after she stood. "I've got to get dinner on for the boys. Let me know how everything goes, will you? I'll be up late studying for a final, so if the light's on, let yourself in."

"I will," Lesley promised.

"Have fun," Daisy said on her way out the door.

That was something Lesley intended to do.

At 6:10, Lesley was standing outside the waterfront aquarium waiting. She glanced at her watch every fifteen seconds, until she saw Chase coming toward her, walking down the hill, his steps hurried and anxious. When he saw her, he raised his hand and waved.

Relief flooded through Lesley. The restless sensation in the pit of her stomach subsided. The doubts that had buffeted against her fled and the painful empty feeling inside her lessened.

"I'm sorry I'm late," he said, after racing across the busy intersection. "I had one hell of a problem finding a place to park."

"It doesn't matter," Lesley said, and it didn't now that he was here. Now that he was grinning at her in a way she found brazenly irresistible.

He looked down on her and said in a low, caressing voice. "You look nice."

"Thank you. You do, too."

"Are you hungry?" he asked.

"A little. How about you?" The foot traffic was heavy and by tacit agreement, they moved to a small fountain and sat on a park bench. She didn't explain that her appetite had been practically nonexistent ever since she'd lost Tony.

"Some, but I've never been to the waterfront before," Chase explained. "Would you mind if we played tourist for a while?"

"I'd love it. Every year I make a point of bringing my class down here. They love the aquarium and the fact that some of the world's largest octopuses live in Elliott Bay. The kids think of them as real monsters."

"From what I understand," Chase said, amused, "the octopuses are actually quite shy."

"I've read that, too, but I wouldn't want to spoil the kids' fun."

They stood and Chase reached for her hand, entwining their fingers. It felt good to be linked to him, although she was sure he was holding her for more practical purposes. The waterfront, at this time of the evening, was teeming with tourists and the two of them could easily have been separated.

"Other than the aquarium, my kids' favorite stop is on Pier 54," she added conversationally.

"What's on Pier 54?"

"A long row of tourist shops. Or in other words, one of the world's largest collections of junk and tacky souvenirs."

"Sounds interesting."

"To third graders it's heaven. Imagine what my parents think when their children come home with a plastic shrunken head with Seattle stamped across the neck. I shouldn't be so flippant, there's some interesting Northwest Indian and Eskimo art on display, if you want to walk that way."

"Sure. What's that?" he asked, pointing toward a large structure beyond the souvenir shops.

"The Washington State Ferries terminal. We have the largest ferry system in the world. I didn't know if you were aware of that or not. If you're looking for a little peace and some beautiful scenery, hop on a ferry. They leave every twenty minutes or so, and if you catch the Winslow Ferry over to Bainbridge Island, it's only a half hour each way, and the ride is marvelous. For a time shortly after Tony told me about April, I used to come down here and take a ferry. There's something about being on the water, of facing the force of the wind and letting it whip around me that greatly soothed my spirit."

"Would you come with me sometime?" Chase asked. "I'd like to stand with you."

"I'd enjoy that very much," she whispered. His hand squeezed hers and she congratulated herself on how even she managed to keep her voice. Countless times over the past few months she'd ridden the ferry, sat with a cup of coffee or stood on the deck. She wasn't sure what it was about being on the water that she found so peaceful, but it helped more than anything else.

They walked along the pier and in and out of several of the tourist shops, chatting as they went. It had been a long time since Lesley had laughed so easily or so often and it felt wonderfully good.

They strolled past the ferry terminal and Lesley asked, "Have you been to Pioneer Square? There's a fabulous restaurant close by if Italian food interests you."

"That sounds great."

"I'll tell you all about Pioneer Square while we eat, then," Lesley said, leading the way. The restaurant was busy, but they were seated after a ten-minute wait.

No sooner were they handed menus than a basket of warm bread was delivered along with a relish tray, overflowing with fresh vegetables and a variety of black and green olives.

"Pioneer Square is actually the oldest part of Seattle," Lesley explained. "It was originally an Indian village, and later a rowdy frontier settlement and gold-rush town."

"What's all the business about mail-order brides?" Chase asked while buttering a thick slice of the bread.

"So you heard about that?"

"I wouldn't have if it hadn't been for a television series that was based on the idea. It ran several years back as I recall."

"The brides are a historical fact. Back in the 1860s, Seattle had a severe shortage of women. In answer to the problem, a well-intended gentleman by the name of Asa Mercer traveled East and recruited a number of New England women to come to Seattle. These weren't ladies of the night, either, but enterprising souls who were well educated, cultured and refined. The ideal type of woman to settle the wild frontier."

"What could Asa Mercer possibly have said to induce these women to give up the comforts of civilization? How'd he induce them to agree to travel to the wild West?" Chase asked, setting aside his bread and focusing his full attention on her.

"It might surprise you to know he didn't have the least bit of difficulty convincing these women. First off, there was a real shortage of marriageable men due to the ravages of the Civil War. Many of these women were facing spinsterhood. Asa Mercer's proposition might well have been their only chance of finding a husband.''

''I see.''

Lesley didn't understand his frown. ''That troubles you?''

''No, no,'' he was quick to assure her. ''Go on, tell me what happened.''

''The first women landed at the waterfront on May 16, 1864. I remember the day so well, because May 16th is my birthday. Seattle was a rip-roaring town and I can imagine these dear women must have wondered what they were letting themselves in for. It didn't take them long, however, to settle in and bring touches of civilization to Seattle. They did such a good job that two years later a second group of brides were imported.''

''They all married then?''

''All but one,'' Lesley explained. ''Lizzie Ordway. Eventually she became the superintendent of public schools and a women's activist. It was because of her and other women like Lizzie that Washington State granted women the right to vote a full ten years ahead of the constitutional amendment.''

''Now you're the one frowning,'' Chase commented.

''I was just thinking that...I don't know,'' she said, feeling foolish.

''What were you thinking?'' Chase asked gently.

She didn't want to say it, didn't want to voice the fears that gnawed at her soul. That she feared she would end up like Lizzie, unmarried and alone. Other than these few details, Lesley knew nothing about the other woman's life. She wondered if Lizzie had found fulfillment in the women's suffrage movement. If she'd found contentment as a spinster, when her friends had married one by one until she was the only one left. The only one who hadn't been able to find a husband. Lizzie stood alone with no one to love and no one to love her.

"Lesley," Chase prompted.

"It's nothing," Lesley insisted, forcing herself to smile, hoping that would assure him.

The waiter came just then, to Lesley's relief, and they ordered. Their dinner was wonderful, but she expected nothing less.

Afterward, they caught the streetcar and returned to the waterfront. While on the short ride, Lesley gave Chase the history of the vintage cars that had been brought from Australia.

"This is Tasmanian mahogany you say?" Chase repeated.

"And white ash wood."

"I'm impressed by how well you know Seattle's history," Chase commented when they climbed off the streetcar.

"I'm a teacher, remember?"

Chase grinned and it was that sexy, make-your-knees-weak sort of smile. "I was just wondering why they didn't have anyone as beautiful as you when I was in school. I was taught by the descendants of Lizzie Ordway."

Lesley laughed, although his words struck close to home. Too close for comfort.

"How about taking that ferry ride?" Chase suggested next.

"Sure." Lesley was game as long as it meant their evening wouldn't end. She didn't want it to be over so soon, especially when she'd done the majority of the talking. There were several questions she wanted to ask Chase about Alaska. Normally Lesley didn't dominate a conversation this way, but Chase seemed genuinely interested.

As luck would have it, the Winslow Ferry was docked and they walked right on. While Lesley found them a table, Chase ordered two cafe lattes.

He slipped into the seat across from her and handed her the paper cup. Lesley carefully pried open the lid and stirred it with the small red straw.

"I've done all the talking," she said, easing back against the padded cushion. "What can you tell me about Alaska?"

"Plenty," he assured her. "Did you know Alaska has the westernmost and easternmost spots in the country?"

"No," Lesley admitted, squinting while she reasoned out how that was possible. She guessed it had something to do with the sweep of islands that stretched nearly to the Asian coastline.

"We've got incredible mountains, too. Seventeen of the twenty highest mountains in the entire United States are in Alaska."

"I love mountains. When we're finished with our drinks, let's stand out on the deck. I want to show you the Olympics. They're so beautiful with their jagged peaks, especially this time of night, just before the sun sets."

A short while later they strolled onto the windswept deck and walked over to the railing. The sun kissed the snowcapped peaks and a pale pink sky, filled with splashes of gold, spilled across the skyline.

"It's a beautiful night," Lesley said, holding on to the railing. The scent of the water was fresh and stimulating. The wind gusted around her, wildly blowing her hair. A couple of times she tried to anchor it behind her ears, but the force of the wind was too strong.

Chase stood behind her in an effort to block the brunt of the gusts. He looped his arms around her shoulders and rested his jaw against the top of her head.

Lesley felt warm and protected in the shelter of his arms. It had a feeling of exquisite peace to be at this place with this man, on this day. This stranger had helped her more in the few hours they'd been together, than all the wisdom and counsel her family and friends had issued in months.

"Let him go," Chase whispered close to her ear.

A thousand times Lesley had tried to do exactly that. More times than she cared to count, more times than her heart wanted to remember. It wasn't only her day-to-day life that was intricately woven with Tony's, but her future, as well. Everything had been centered around their lives together. She couldn't walk into her home and not be confronted by the evidence of their three-year courtship.

The bookcases in her living room had been purchased with Tony. They'd picked out the sofa and love seat together, and a hundred other things, as well. Even her wardrobe had been bought with him in mind. The dress she was wearing this evening had been purchased for Tony for a special dinner they shared.

"I want to go back in now," she said stiffly, and wondered if Chase could hear her or if he'd chosen to ignore her request. "It's getting chilly."

He released her reluctantly, Lesley could tell, and in other circumstances his hesitation would have thrilled her. But not now, not when it felt as if her heart were melting inside her and she was fighting back a fresh stab of pain.

"I'm sorry," she said when they returned to their seats.

"Don't be," Chase said gently. "I shouldn't have pressured you."

Lesley struggled for the words to explain her pain, but she could find none. She'd found her grief to be as black as coal, filled with musty shadows and darker corners. Some days it resembled fire, burning at her confidence, charring the walls of her self-esteem. Other days, it was a long, windy path, filled with the hopeless ruts of self-pity, disappointment and shame. The worst part of traveling this road was that she'd been so alone, so lost and so terribly afraid.

The ferry docked at Winslow and they walked off and waited in the terminal, before boarding again. Neither seemed to be in the mood to talk, but it was a peaceful kind of silence. Lesley felt no compulsion to fill it with mindless dialogue and apparently neither did Chase.

By the time they arrived back at the Seattle waterfront, the sun had set. Chase held her hand as they rode the walkway down to the street level, his mind in turmoil. He should never have asked Lesley to let go of the man she loved. It had been a mistake to have pressured her and one he had no intention of repeating.

"Where are we going?" she asked as he led her down the pier. The crowds remained thick, the traffic along the sidewalk heavy even at this time of night. The scents of fried fish and the sea mingled in the air.

"Down there," he said, pointing to the length of a deserted pier.

It was a testament of her trust that she didn't hesitate. "There's nothing down there."

"I know. I'm going to kiss you, Lesley, and I prefer to do it without half of Seattle watching me."

"Aren't you taking a good deal for granted?" she asked, more amused than offended.

"Perhaps." But that didn't stop him.

Not giving her the opportunity to argue, he brought her with him and paused only when he was assured of their privacy. Without a word more, he turned her so that she faced him. He captured her hands and guided them upward and around his neck. He felt a moment of hesitation, a second of resistance, but both were quickly gone, both were quickly quelled.

He circled her waist with his arms and pulled her to him. At the feel of her silken body next to his, Chase sighed and marveled when Lesley did, too. Hers was a little sigh. One that said she wasn't sure she was doing the right thing.

He smelled the faint flowery scent of her and felt her breasts flatten against his chest. It was a sensual moment, their bodies pressed against each other, his sex boldly meshed with her femininity. It was a spiritual moment, as well, with two lost souls reaching toward each other, with two lost hearts pounding in unison.

For a long moment, they simply held each other. Chase had never spent time with a woman like this. It wasn't his desire that prompted him to take her into his arms. It was something far stronger that he couldn't put words to, something far deeper than the conscious level.

He longed to protect Lesley, shield her from more pain, and at the same time he was looking to her to cure the loneliness of his soul.

Together they stood, two lost and hurting souls against the cold winds of pain and fear and indifference. Against the unspeakable realities of life.

Although Lesley wasn't crying, he felt her tears. They were bottled up inside her.

Chase waged a debate on what to do next, kiss her as he claimed or hold her against him, comfort her for a few moments and then release her.

He couldn't not taste her. Not when she felt so damn good in his arms.

Slowly he lowered his head, giving her ample opportunity to turn away from him. His heart felt as if it would burst wide open when she closed her eyes and brought her mouth to his.

Chase wanted this kiss, wanted it more intensely than he could remember wanting anything. The wanting scared him and he brushed his lips briefly over hers. It was a light kiss, the kind of kiss a woman gives a man when she's teasing him. The kind a man gives a woman when he's looking for a way to not kiss her.

Or when he's afraid he's going to want her too much.

He should have known it wouldn't have been enough to satisfy either of them. Lesley blinked uncertainly and he tried again, this time with sips and nibbles of her slightly parted lips.

This wasn't enough, either. If anything, it created a need for more. Much more.

The third time he kissed her, he opened his mouth and sank his lips onto hers and as the kiss deepened and blossomed, Chase realized he'd made another mistake. The hollow feeling in his stomach returned; the feeling that fate was about to knock him for a loop was back.

Sensation after sensation rippled over him and his sigh was replaced with a groan. Not a deep sexual groan of need or desire, but of awakening. He felt both excited and terrified. Anxious and scared out of his wits. He felt as if he'd leapt off a cliff into the dark and didn't know where he'd land. That, like so much else in life, was left to the unknown.

Lesley groaned, too, and tightened her hold on him. She felt it, too. She must have.

His hands bracketed her face as he lifted his head. This wasn't what he expected or wanted. Emotion came at him in tidal waves. He'd feared this would happen, that he'd be hungry for her, so hungry that it demanded every ounce of fortitude he possessed not to claim her lips again.

They drew apart as if each were aware they had reached the limit, that continuing meant they would go farther than either of them was prepared to deal with just then. Their bottom lips clung with reluctance and they pressed their foreheads together.

"I..." He paused, not finding any words that adequately conveyed his feelings.

Lesley closed her eyes and his nose brushed hers, easing his lips closer to the sweetest temptation he'd ever known.

"I want to see you again," Chase said once he found his voice, once he knew he could speak without making a fool of himself.

"All right" came her breathless reply.

"A movie?" That was the first thing that came to his mind, although it was singularly unimaginative.

"When?"

"Tomorrow." Waiting any longer than a few hours would have been a test of his patience.

"Okay. What time?"

He didn't know. It seemed a bit presumptuous to suggest a matinee, but waiting any longer than noon to see her again seemed impossible.

"I'll give you my phone number," she said.

"I'll call you in the morning and we can talk then."

"Yes," she agreed.

"I'll walk you to your car."

He didn't dare take hold her hand or touch her. He'd never felt this way with a woman, as if he'd lose control with a simple brush of her lips against his. All she needed to do was to sigh that soft womanly sigh that said she wanted him and it would have been all over, right then and there.

They didn't need to walk far. Lesley had parked in a slot beneath the viaduct across the street from the aquarium. He lingered outside her door.

"Thank you," she whispered, not looking at him.

"Dinner was my pleasure."

"I didn't mean for the dinner." She looked at him then and he saw for himself her meaning. She raised her hand and pressed it against his face, then softly, unexpectedly pressed her mouth to his.

"I . . . don't know if I'd have made it through this day without you."

He wanted to deny that. She was strong, far stronger than she gave herself credit for. And resourceful.

"I'm glad I could help," he said finally, when he could think of no way of explaining the strength he read in her without making it sound trite. He longed to reassure her that the man she loved had been a fool to let her go, but she didn't want to hear that, either. Those were the words others had said to her, the counsel friends and family had issued.

"I'll wait to hear from you," she said, unlocking her car door.

He'd be waiting, too, until a respectable amount of time had lapsed so he could phone her.

"Thank you again," she said, silently communicating far more. She closed the door and started the engine. Chase stepped aside as she pulled out of the parking space. He waited until her car had disappeared into the night before he walked to his own.

A smile came to him. He'd made a tactical error by asking Lesley to release the man she loved. But he'd made up for it later when he'd asked her to hold on to him.

She'd clung to him and it had made all the difference in the world.

Chapter Three

The phone rang at eight the following morning. Chase had been up for hours, had eaten breakfast and leisurely read the morning paper. After years of rising early, he never had learned to sleep past six.

The phone pealed a second time. It couldn't possibly be Lesley; he hadn't mentioned the name of the hotel where he was staying, and yet he couldn't keep his heart from hoping it was her.

"Hello," he answered crisply.

"Mr. Goodman, this is the answering service." The woman sounded impatient and more than a little frazzled.

"Someone responded to the ad," Chase guessed. He had nearly forgotten about the billboard.

"*Someone!*" the woman burst out impatiently. "We've had nearly five hundred calls in the last twenty-four hours, including inquiries from two television stations, the *Seattle Times* and four radio stations. Our staff wasn't equipped to deal with this kind of response.''

''Five hundred calls.'' Chase was shocked. He'd never dreamed his advertisement would receive such an overwhelming response.

''Our operators have been bombarded with inquiries, Mr. Goodman.''

''How can I possibly answer so many calls?'' The mere thought of being expected to contact that many women on his own was overpowering.

''I suggest you hire a secretary to weed through the replies. I'm sorry, but I don't think any of us dreamed there would be such an uncontrollable number.''

''You!'' Chase was astonished himself. ''I'll make the arrangements first thing this morning.''

''We'd appreciate it if you'd come and collect the messages as soon as possible.''

''I'll be down directly,'' Chase promised.

Five hundred responses, he mused after he replaced the receiver. It seemed incredible. Absurd. Unbelievable. He didn't know there were that many women who'd even consider such a thing. From what he learned from the answering service, the calls hadn't stopped, either. There were more coming in every minute.

He reached for his car keys and was ready to leave when a knock sounded. When he opened the door, he discovered a newswoman and a man with a camera on the other side.

''You're Chase Goodman?'' the woman asked. She was slight and pretty and he recognized her from the newscast the night before. She was a TV reporter, and although he couldn't remember her name, her face was familiar.

"I'm Chase Goodman," he answered, eyeing the man with the camera. "What can I do for you?"

"The same Chase Goodman who rented the billboard off Denny Way?"

"Yes."

She smiled then. "I'm Becky Bright from KYGN-TV and this is Steve Dalton, my cameraman. Would you mind if I asked you a few questions? I promise we won't take much of your time."

Chase couldn't see any harm in that, but he didn't like the idea of someone sticking a camera in his face. He hesitated and then decided, "I suppose that would be all right."

"Great." The reporter walked into his hotel room, pulled out a chair and instructed Chase to sit down. He did, but he didn't take his eye off the cameraman. A series of bright lights nearly blinded him.

"Sorry," Becky said apologetically. "I should have warned you about the glare. Now, tell me, Mr. Goodman, what prompted you to advertise for a wife?"

Chase held up his hand to shield his eyes from the blinding light. "Ah . . . I'm from Alaska."

"Alaska," she repeated, reaching for his arm and lowering it away from his face.

"I'm only going to be in town a few weeks and I wanted to make the most of my time," he elaborated, squinting. "It seemed like a good idea if I was going to find a wife to be as straightforward about it as I could be. I didn't want there to be any misunderstanding of my intentions."

"Have you had any responses?"

Chase remained incredulous. "I just got off the phone with the answering service and they've been flooded with calls. They said there've been over five hundred."

"That surprises you?"

"You're damn right it does. I figured I'd be lucky to find more than a handful of women willing to move just outside of Prudhoe Bay."

"The women who've applied know this?"

"Yes. I left the pertinent details of who I am and what a woman can expect if they married me, with the answering service as a screening technique. Only those who were willing to accept the conditions I mentioned were to leave their name and phone number."

"And five hundred had done that?"

"Apparently so. I was on my way to the agency just now."

"How do you intend to interview five hundred or more women?"

Chase rubbed his hand against the side of his jaw. This situation was quickly getting out of hand. "I'm hoping to hire a secretary as soon as I can. This whole thing has gone much further than I expected."

"If you were to speak to the women who've answered your advertisement, what would you say?"

Chase wasn't one who thought well on his feet, especially when he was cornered by a fast-talking reporter and a cameraman who seemed intent on blinding him. "I guess I'd ask them to be patient. I promise to respond to every call, but it might take me a few days."

"Will you be holding interviews yourself?"

Chase hadn't thought this far ahead. His original idea had been to meet each applicant for dinner, get to know one another in a nonthreatening, casual atmosphere, and then proceed, depending on how they felt about him and how he felt about them. All that had changed now. "I suspect I'll be meeting them personally," he said reluctantly.

Becky stood and the lights immediately dimmed. "It's been a pleasure talking to you, Mr. Goodman. We'll be running this on the noon news and later on the five o'clock edition, if you're interested in seeing yourself on television."

"So soon?"

"We might even do a follow-up report after you've selected your bride, but I'll have to wait until I talk that over with my producer. We'd appreciate an exclusive. Can we count on you for that?"

"Ah...sure."

"Great." She beamed him a game-show-host smile.

"Before you go," Chase said, gathering his wits, "how'd you know where to find me?" He'd purposely set up the answering service to avoid this very thing.

"Easy," Becky said, sticking her pad and pen inside her purse. "I contacted the billboard company. They told me where to reach you."

Chase opened the door for the two, feeling very much like a fool. He should never have agreed to the interview. They'd caught him off guard, before he realized what he was doing. If anything, this meeting was likely to generate additional calls and he already had more than he knew how to deal with.

Chase slumped onto the end of the bed. He'd tried to be honest and fair. He wanted a wife; he needed a woman's gentleness in his life. For thirty-three years he'd been content to live and work alone, waiting until he could offer a woman a decent life. No longer.

The shortage of women in Alaska was well-known, especially in the frozen north. When Lesley had told him the details of the Seattle brides back in the 1860s, he felt a certain kinship with Asa Mercer and those desperate, lonely men who'd put up the money for such a venture.

Lesley had told him Mercer hadn't much difficulty convincing the women to move west. That had surprised him, but not as much as the response his own ad had generated.

Lesley.

Her name went through his mind like a sharp blade and he wiped his hand down his face as the dread settled over him. He'd meant to tell her about the billboard that first afternoon. But then she'd mentioned it herself and claimed anyone who'd advertise for a wife was a crazy man. He feared she'd never have agreed to their dinner date had she known he was that man.

He reached for the phone, intending to call her right then and clear the air. He fumbled for her phone number inside his wallet and spread it out on the bed stand. After punching four numbers in quick succession, he changed his mind and replaced the receiver. This sort of thing was best said face-to-face. He only hoped she'd be more inclined to think well of him now that she knew him better.

He'd wait until a decent hour and contact her, he decided. His one concern was that she didn't watch the noon news, otherwise he was sure to lose her.

Lesley woke happy. At least she thought this feeling was happiness. All she knew was that she'd slept the entire night through and when morning arrived, the dark heavy cloud of despair that had followed her the past few months had lifted. Her heart felt lighter, her head clearer and her spirit whole.

She wasn't falling in love with Chase. Not by a long shot. But he'd helped her look past the cloud of pain she'd been walking under; he'd eased her toward the light. With Chase she'd laughed again and for that alone she would always be grateful.

She showered and after fiddling with her hair, twisting it into a thick French braid, she brewed a pot of coffee. While reading through the morning paper, she decided to bake chocolate-chip cookies. Eric and Kevin, Daisy's two boys, would be thrilled.

Chase might enjoy them, as well.

Chase.

She smiled as she poised the coffee cup in front of her lips, her elbows braced against the kitchen table. It didn't do any good to kid herself. She was baking those cookies for him. Later she'd suggest an outing to Paradise on Mount Rainier.

True, Eric and Kevin would appreciate a share, but it was Chase she was hoping to impress. Chase she was looking forward to hearing from again. Chase who dominated her thoughts all morning.

The cookies were cooling on the counter on wax paper when Daisy arrived.

"What are you doing home so early?" Lesley asked, pleased to see her friend, as always.

"I got through with the test early. Say, what's going on here?" she asked, helping herself to a warm cookie.

"I don't know. I felt the urge to bake this morning."

Daisy pulled out a chair and dropped her thick computer books on the table. "It's the nesting instinct taking root. Mark my word, sweetie, those ole hormones are kicking in."

Lesley paused, her hand holding a spatula that was weighted down with a cookie. "I beg your pardon?"

"You're how old now? Twenty-five, twenty-six?"

"Twenty-six," Lesley admitted.

"Your friends are mostly married. You've probably got a dozen or so girlfriends with kids of their own. Some with two and three kids, right?"

"Yes," Lesley admitted, agreeably enough, "but that doesn't mean anything."

"Who are you trying to fool? Not me! As far as I'm concerned, marriage and a family were the big attraction you felt for Tony. He was never your type and we both know it. What you were looking forward to was settling down, getting pregnant and doing the mother thing."

"We agreed not to discuss Tony, remember," Lesley reminded her neighbor stiffly. Her former fiancé was a subject she chose to avoid whenever possible with her friends, especially with Daisy, who'd insisted from the first Tony was all wrong for her.

"You agreed *we* wouldn't," Daisy muttered, chewing the cookie, "but I'll respect your wishes as long as you fill me in on your date last night."

Lesley smiled. "Ah, yes, my date."

"You must have gotten back late. I wasn't through studying until well after midnight and I didn't hear you come home."

Lesley hadn't stopped to chat with Daisy, fearing that sharing her experience would somehow diminish her time with Chase. She'd gone to bed almost immediately, wanting to mull over their time together, put some perspective on it, discern what she could.

Their kisses had touched a deep part of her and left her feeling warm and whole. She'd intended to think through all that. Instead, she'd fallen asleep almost immediately. Even now she wasn't sure what to read into their evening together.

"Did you have a good time?" Daisy pressed.

"Wonderful. We walked along the waterfront, and then went to dinner." She didn't mention the ferry ride. She couldn't. It was too special to share even with Daisy.

All morning she'd worked at shutting out the memory of Chase's kiss and the wealth of feeling just thinking about it created. She hadn't experienced those emotions in so very long.

She wasn't sure what had happened between them, only that something had. Whatever it was, she'd allowed it. Had fully participated in it, and in the end could find no way to deny him or herself the pleasure of those few kisses.

No one had ever kissed her the way Chase had, gently, with such infinite care, with such tenderness. He'd kissed her the way a woman dreams of being kissed, dreams of being held. Sharing that, ever trying to explain it, was beyond Lesley. She wouldn't even know where to begin.

Daisy yawned with great exaggeration. "It sounds like a perfectly boring date if you ask me."

"Maybe, but I've never had two men fight with switchblades over me the way you did. It's straight downhill from there as far as I'm concerned."

"Both men were staggering drunk. Besides, I had no intention of dating either one of them. After being married to Brent for five years, why would I want to involve myself with another biker wannabe? Charlie had the police there so fast my head spun. Good thing, too."

Personally, Lesley believed the bartender was sweet on Daisy, but she'd never said as much. Charlie was a nice guy and he looked out for her neighbor, but to Lesley's way of thinking, he had more than a soft spot in his heart for the cocktail waitress.

"Don't sidetrack me," Daisy insisted. "We were talking about you and Chase. That was his name, wasn't it?"

Lesley nodded. "There's not much more to say. I already told you I had a nice time."

"I believe you described it as 'wonderful.' You seeing him again?"

"We're going to a movie this evening...at least I think we are. He first mentioned it last night, but he didn't say anything about it when he phoned a few minutes ago."

"So he's already called again?"

Lesley tried not to show how pleased she was. Chase had sounded distracted, but there was no disguising the warmth in his voice. Whatever was plaguing him was temporary, she felt, and he sounded as though speaking to her those few minutes were the link to his sanity. She hoped he'd tell her whatever was troubling him when he picked her up that evening. He'd asked for her address and Lesley had no qualms about giving it to him.

"What's this?" Daisy asked, reaching across the table to a stack of mail and pulling out a catalog.

"A needlepoint catalog," Lesley said, stacking the cookie sheets into her sink to cool.

"When did you start this?" Daisy asked, slowly flipping through the pages.

"A couple of months ago."

"The nesting instinct strikes again."

"Don't be ridiculous," Lesley countered, growing impatient. She walked onto her back porch, retrieved an empty coffee can and filled it with cookies. "Here," she said, thrusting the can toward her smart-mouthed neighbor. "For Eric and Kevin."

Chuckling, Daisy stood, reached for her books and the cookies. "I can take a hint. You don't want me talking about Tony and you don't want me mentioning your ripening hormones, either. It's getting downright difficult to carry on a conversation with you, girl."

After shooing Daisy out the door, Lesley made herself a sandwich and turned on the local noon news. She was chewing away on her lunch when the billboard she'd seen earlier that week came on the screen.

Her interest was piqued.

The camera left the billboard to focus on the reporter who was standing below it. Generally, Lesley liked Becky Bright and the offbeat stories she reported. It was a compliment to her professionalism as far as Lesley was concerned that Becky Bright could cover the billboard story and keep a straight face.

"I talked this morning with the man who's so earnestly seeking a wife," Becky announced. "Chase Goodman agreed to an interview and..."

Chase Goodman.

Lesley didn't hear a word beyond that. Chase's face came onto the screen and he squinted into the camera and announced he only had a limited time in Seattle and wanted to be as straightforward as he could.

Straightforward. He'd misled *her*. Talk about being unethical; why he'd... he'd kissed her. He'd held her in his arms and... Mortified, she pressed her hands to her face. She'd so desperately wanted to believe in Chase, but he was like all the other men she'd known. He was just like her father, who'd cruelly deceived her. Just like Tony, who'd broken her heart. Never again would she make herself vulnerable. Never again would she trust her own judgment.

Never again.

"Your next appointment is waiting," Sandra Zielger, the attractive middle-aged woman Chase had hired that morning, announced. He'd been interviewing women all afternoon.

The first one who'd come was a pleasant woman a few years his senior who worked as an executive secretary for a big manufacturing company. She was congenial, well educated and professional. When Chase asked her about why she wanted to marry him and move to Alaska, she claimed she was ready to get out of the rat race and take life at a more leisurely pace. She'd been twice divorced, with no children. After ten minutes with her, Chase knew a relationship between them wouldn't work. He wasn't comfortable with her the way he was with Lesley.

The second interview turned out to be with a woman plumber who'd been working construction. She'd been out of work for three months and was looking for a change of scene. The first thing she asked him was if he wanted to sleep with her first to sample the goods before making his decision. Even before he collected his wits enough to respond, she'd unbuttoned her blouse, claiming she didn't mind a little kinky sex if that interested him, but she wasn't overly fond of whips and chains. By the time he'd ushered her out the door, Chase felt shaken to the core.

He wasn't sure what he'd expected when he'd placed the ad, but it wasn't this. He was looking for a woman with a generous heart, one with pluck and spirit. A woman with depth and sensitivity. A woman like... Lesley.

He rubbed his hand along the back of his neck, closed his eyes and sighed.

He tried phoning Lesley just to calm his nerves, but she wasn't home. He didn't leave a message on her machine because he was uncomfortable with those silly contraptions.

By four, Chase had talked with so many women that their names and faces and their stories had all started to blend together. Not a single one had struck his fancy. He couldn't meet with these women and not compare them to Lesley. They seemed shallow by contrast, frivolous and, in some cases, reckless. There were a couple he might have liked to know under other circumstances, and he'd kept their names and phone numbers, but not a single woman to compare to the one he'd met yesterday, quite by chance.

He glanced at his watch and knew he wasn't up to interviewing another woman. The suite he'd rented at the hotel was packed with applicants. The word had gotten out that he was in the process of talking to prospective brides and they were coming in off the streets now. Sandra Zielger, his secretary, seemed to have her hands full, and seeing that, Chase intervened, escorting the husband-seeking women from the room with promises of another day.

"I've never seen anything like this," Sandra said, pushing the hair away from her face with both hands. "You should have brought some of your bachelor friends along with you."

Chase closed his eyes and expelled a weary sigh. "How many women did we see?"

"Twenty."

"That's all?" He felt the panic rise. He'd spent nearly one entire day meeting with and talking to women from all walks of life, and he hadn't so much as made a dent in those who'd expressed interest in him.

"I take it you're finished for the day?" Sandra asked.

Chase nodded. He needed space to breathe and time to think. What he really needed, Chase realized, was Lesley. He hadn't stopped thinking about her all day, or about the kisses they'd shared. Nor could he forget how soft and warm she'd felt in his arms. Nor could he keep from wanting to hold her again and soon.

He was halfway out the door when Sandra stopped him. "You're not leaving, are you?"

"You mean I can't?"

"Well, I'm not one to say. It's just that there are several phone messages that need to be returned."

"From whom?"

"The radio stations for one. Another television station."

"Forget them. That last thing I need now is more publicity."

Sandra grinned and removed the pen tucked behind her ear. "I've had several interesting jobs working for Temp Help over the years, but I've got to tell you, this is the most unusual. I wish you luck, young man."

"Thanks," Chase answered. He had the distinct feeling he was going to need it.

Lesley had been filled with nervous energy from the moment she'd seen Becky Bright stand beneath that ridiculous billboard and say Chase's name. None of the usual remedies to work out her aggression had worked.

She'd gone shopping and fifteen minutes later stormed out of the store. She was too mad to appreciate a fifty-percent-off sale. That was anger so rare it surprised even her.

A long soak in the tub hadn't helped, either. By the time she'd finished, she'd sloshed water all over the floor and had spilled her favorite liquid bubble bath.

Even a Jane Fonda fitness tape didn't help, but then she'd stopped five minutes into the exercises and turned if off. If she was going to do anything aerobic, Lesley decided, she'd prefer to work in her yard.

She weeded the front flower beds and was watering the bright red geraniums with her hose when Daisy walked out of the house in the shortest pair of shorts and the skimpiest top Lesley had ever seen. Her heels added a full two inches to her height.

"You upset about something, honey?" she called over the white picket fence that divided their property.

"What makes you ask that?" Lesley returned in a completely reasonable voice. That Daisy was able to read how upset she was fueled her already shortened temper.

"It could be that you're nearly drowning those poor flowers. They need to be watered like a gentle rainfall and not with hurricane force."

"Oh," Lesley murmured, realizing her neighbor was right.

"The boys thank you for the cookies."

"Tell them I've got a cookie jarful that they're welcome to, as well."

"I thought you'd baked those cookies for Chase."

"I never said that." Lesley was sure she hadn't.

"Of course you did, not verbally, but it was obvious. You like this guy and you aren't going to fool me into thinking otherwise. All I can say is great. It's about time you got over that two-timing, no-good bum."

"Chase isn't any better," Lesley insisted, continuing with her watering efforts, concentrating on her lawn.

"What makes you say that?"

"You know that billboard off Denny Way that's causing all the commotion?" Lesley asked.

"The one with the guy advertising for a bride?" It must have clicked in Daisy's mind all at once because she snapped her fingers and pointed at Lesley. "That's Chase?"

"The very one."

"And that's bad?"

"The man's a loony," Lesley insisted.

"You didn't think so earlier in the day. Fact is, you were as happy as I've seen you in a good long while."

"That was before I knew. He goes on TV and claims the reason he decided on the billboard was so he could be direct and honest. He wasn't either one with me."

"You've got to trust your instincts," Daisy advised thoughtfully, "and you had a wonderful time with him earlier."

Now Lesley had heard everything. "Trust my instincts? I was engaged to a man who wasn't even in love with me and I didn't figure it out until half the school knew, including the student body." It mortified her to remember the strange, sympathetic looks she'd gotten from her peers weeks prior to her broken engagement.

"Stop blaming yourself for that," Daisy said, placing her hands on her hips. "You didn't suspect Tony because you shouldn't have suspected him. Trust me, honey, you got the better end of the deal in that affair. Mark my words. Two or three years down the road, he's going to get a roving eye again. It's a pattern with certain men. I've seen it before, plenty of times."

"Tony's not like that," Lesley insisted. Even after all this time she couldn't keep from defending him. After all this time she'd couldn't keep herself from loving him. The first ray of hope had happened with Chase, and now that was challenged by his deception.

"It seems to me that there's more to Chase than meets the eye," Daisy said thoughtfully. "You have to admit he's innovative."

"The man rented a billboard and advertised for a wife," Lesley cried. "That's not innovation, that's stupidity."

"He shows initiative, too."

"How can you defend him when you haven't even met him?"

"You're right, of course," Daisy was quick to agree, "but there's something about him I like. He can't be so bad, otherwise you'd never have gone out with him."

"That was before I knew what he really was like."

"The guy's obviously got money. Did you ever stop to think about that? Billboards don't come cheap."

"Money's never interested me."

"It doesn't unless you need it," Daisy answered with a twinge of sarcasm. "Another thing . . ."

"You mean there's more?"

"There's always more. This guy is serious. He isn't going to string you along the way you-know-who did. Good grief, you dated the-guy-you-don't-want-me-to-mention how many years?"

"Three."

"That's what I thought. There's a distinct advantage in knowing what a guy wants from you. Chase doesn't have a hidden agenda."

"Everything you say is true, but it doesn't discount the fact he deceived me."

"Just a minute." Daisy was wagging her index finger at her again. "Didn't you tell me Chase ran after the man who stole your purse? It isn't any man who'd willingly become involved in something like that. Did you ever stop to think that mugger might have had a gun?"

Lesley had raced after him herself and the thought had completely escaped her. Apparently it had escaped Chase, too.

"It isn't every man who's willing to put his life on the line in order to help another human being."

"If the mugger had owned a gun, he would have used it to get my purse. Instead he was just clever." Now that the matter was settled, Lesley was free once more to be furious with Chase. She didn't want to think of him as a hero, even if he had gotten her purse back for her. The action had been instinctive and nothing more.

"I'm offering you some advice," Daisy said.

"Are you going to give it to me whether I want it or not?"

"Probably."

"Then fire away."

"Don't be so quick to judge Chase. He sounds like the decent sort to me, and one hell more of a man than—"

"I thought we weren't going to discuss Tony again."

Daisy shook her head as if saddened by Lesley's lack of insight as far as men were concerned. Her eyes brightened as she looked toward the road. "What type of car did you say Chase drives?"

"I didn't. Why?"

"Because one hunk of a guy just pulled up in a red truck."

Lesley whirled around to find Chase climbing out of the four-wheel-drive vehicle. His smile rivaled the sun as his eyes fell on her watering the lawn.

"I haven't come at a bad time, have I?" he called out from the driveway.

Chapter Four

"Hey," Daisy whispered as Chase approached, "this guy is gorgeous. You don't happen to remember the phone number on that billboard, do you? I think *I'll* apply."

Lesley cast her neighbor a scalding look.

"Not!" Daisy laughed, thinking herself amusing.

"I take it you saw the noon news," Chase said cautiously.

"You mean the story about the crazy billboard. Yes, I saw it."

Chase took a couple of cautious steps toward her. "Are you going to squirt me with that hose?"

"I should." It was a credit to her upbringing that she didn't do exactly that.

Angry shouts burst from Daisy's house and Eric chased Kevin out the front door. Lesley's neighbor cursed and shouted for the two boys to stop fighting. It soon became obvious that she was needed to untangle her sons.

"Damn," Daisy said, "and I was hoping to hear this." She stepped forward and shook hands with Chase. "I'm Lesley's neighbor. Be patient with her. She'll come around."

"Daisy!" It irritated Lesley no end that her friend would side with Chase and worse, offer him advice on how to handle her.

"I'll talk to you later," Daisy said as she walked back over to her house, her high heels clapping against the cement walkway.

"I would have said something yesterday," Chase told her, keeping a safe distance between them. "But you mentioned having seen the billboard yourself, remember?"

Lesley lowered her eyes. She'd forgotten about that. She'd more than mentioned the billboard, she'd offered a detailed opinion of the mental state of the man who'd paid for it, never guessing it was Chase.

"You could have told me later, after dinner," she reminded him. "That would have been the fair thing to do."

Chase advanced one step. "You're right, I should have, but honest to God, Lesley, it completely slipped my mind. I got so caught up with being with you that I forgot. I realize that's a poor excuse, but it's the truth."

Lesley felt herself weakening. She'd enjoyed their evening together, too. That was what hurt so much now. For the first time in months she'd been able to shed the hurt of Tony's betrayal and have fun. Playing the role of tour guide and showing Chase the city she loved had freed her soul. After she'd seen the noon news, all those reawakened emotions felt like a sham. Instead of anticipation, she'd suffered regret.

"I was hoping you'd agree to see me again," Chase said, enticingly. "I've been meeting with women all day and I haven't met a single one I like as well as you."

"Of course you like me the best," Lesley cried indignantly. "Only a crazy woman would answer that ad."

Chase buried his hands in his pants pockets. "That's what you said when you mentioned the ad, remember? You had me wondering, but Lesley, you're wrong. I've spent the entire afternoon meeting with them, and that isn't the case. Most have been pleasant and sincere."

"Then you should be dating them." Her miniature lawn was well past the point of being watered, but she persisted, drenching it. If she continued, it'd soon be swampland.

"You're probably right. I should be getting to know them better. But I'd rather spend my free time with you. Will you have dinner with me tonight?"

The temptation was strong, but Lesley refused to give in to it. "I . . . don't think so."

"Why not?"

"Something's come up unexpectedly."

"What?" Chase pressed.

"I forgot I was meeting a friend."

"That's not very original, Lesley. Try again."

"Don't do this," she pleaded.

"Where would you like to eat?"

"I said I couldn't."

"Any restaurant in town—you name it."

Lesley hadn't expected him to persevere. She could be equally stubborn. A rejection had already formed in her mind, when Chase removed the hose from her hand, took her by the shoulders and turned her to face him. She might have been able to send him away if he hadn't touched her, but the moment he did, Lesley knew this was going to be far more difficult than it should be.

Lesley knew the exact second she surrendered; it was the same moment she realized he was going to kiss her and how badly she wanted him to.

His palms framed her face and he took her mouth with a greedy kind of tenderness. Not only did Lesley allow the kiss, but she assisted him. Her hands splayed across his chest and she leaned closer, opening her mouth to him. His tongue slipped inside, hot and fiery, and touched hers in bold ways that set her heart to thudding like a giant drum against her ribs. His kiss was hungry and demanding and her clenched fists knotted the fabric of his shirt as she battled against the strong undertow of sensation. By the time it ended, Lesley knew she'd lost.

"Do you believe in fate?" he whispered, his moist mouth rubbing hers.

"I ... I don't think so."

"I didn't until I met you."

"Stop, Chase. Please ..." She was fighting him for all she was worth and losing more ground for every second he held her.

"Dinner. That's all I ask. One last time together and if you decide afterward that you don't want to see me again, then fine."

"Promise?"

"Cross my heart and hope to die."

Despite the massive doses of indecision she was dealing with, Lesley laughed.

"Now where would you like to eat? Anyplace in town, just name it."

"Ah ..."

"The Space Needle? Canlis? Il Bistro?"

It was apparent he fully intended to wine and dine her, but Lesley knew a much better way of testing a man's character than sitting across from him in some fancy restaurant with a handful of attentive waiters seeing to their every need.

"I'd like to eat at Charlie's Burgers and then play a game of golf."

Chase's eyes widened. "Golf?"

"You heard me."

"Lesley, sweetheart, I don't know if you realize this or not, but there isn't a golf course within eight hundred miles of Twin Creeks. I've never played the game."

"You'll pick it up real fast, I'm sure. Those are my conditions. Take them or leave them."

Chase groaned and rubbed his hand down his face. "All right, if you want to see me make a fool of myself."

Miniature golf. That was what Lesley had in mind.

She'd left him to stew and worry all the way through their hamburgers before they drove to the golf course and he learned the full truth. It was just punishment, he decided, for what he'd put her through.

To his surprise, Lesley was quite good at it, soundly defeating him on the first nine holes. But as she claimed, he was a fast learner, rallying in the last nine holes. When they added up their scores, Lesley won by three strokes.

"I can't remember the last time I laughed so much," she admitted over a glass of ice tea. They were relaxing on the patio under a pink-and-orange-striped umbrella, surrounded by children and a handful of adults. "You're a good sport, Chase."

"Does that surprise you?"

She hesitated. "A little. Men don't like to lose, especially to a woman."

"That's not true in all situations, just some."

"Name one." Her challenge was there, bold as could be.

"When it comes to a woman deciding between two men," he answered thoughtfully. "Naturally, I can't speak for all men, but there's one thing that bothers me more than anything."

"And that's?"

"When I'm forced to compete with another man for a woman's affection."

Lesley grew quiet after that and Chase hoped he hadn't offended her with his honesty. He couldn't apologize for speaking the truth.

"Tell me about the women you saw today," she said unexpectedly, sounding almost cheerful. He caught the gleam in her eye and he realized she was prepared to hear horror stories.

"I was surprised, really surprised by some."

"Oh? Were they that awful?"

"No," he countered quickly, "Not at all—there were some classy women in the group, with good educations. One of the first I interviewed had her master's degree."

"What prompted her to respond to your ad?" The self-satisfied look disappeared, replaced by one of genuine curiosity.

Chase had wondered about that himself. "I asked about her motives right off. Don't get me wrong—Twin Creeks is a nice, civilized town, but it's a long way from shopping centers, large libraries and cultural events. You aren't ever going to see any Broadway shows performed there. I explained all that to Mary."

"And she still wanted to marry you?"

Chase nodded. "At least she said she did. When it came right down to it, she's over thirty and the years have slipped by without her noticing. Now she realizes how badly she wants a husband and family. She claimed every guy she's dated in the last few years is either emotionally and mentally scarred from dating or a divorce. Or both."

"Having recently reentered the dating scene myself, I'm beginning to realize how true that is."

"Mary is mainly interested in starting a family," Chase concluded.

"How do you feel about children?" She braced her elbows against the table and rested her chin in her palms as she studied him.

"I want a family, but I'd prefer to wait a year or two, to give my wife the opportunity to know me better and for me to know her. To my way of thinking, it's important to be certain the marriage is going to last before we bring a child into the equation."

"That's an intelligent way to look at it."

Lesley went silent again and he saw pain bleed into her eyes and wondered at the cause. He was about to question her about it when she spoke again.

"Other than Mary, is there another woman that sticks out in your mind?"

"Several. A female plumber who let me know she doesn't mind kinky sex."

The look that came over Lesley was very prim and proper. "I see."

"And Bunny, who has four children under the age of six."

"Oh my goodness."

"She was looking for someone to help her raise her children and was honest about it. Her husband abandoned her with the kids nine months ago."

"The rat."

Chase agreed with her. "I don't understand how a man can walk away from his responsibilities like that. It's bad enough that he wounded Bunny's soul, but to leave those beautiful children."

"She brought them?"

"No, I asked to see a picture. They're towheads and cute as could be. I felt sorry for her." He didn't mention that he'd given her enough money to fill her gas tank so she could get home. She hadn't asked, but he knew she was in dire financial straits.

"You aren't interested in a woman with excess baggage?" she asked, almost flippantly. Though he only knew Lesley a short time, he already knew that it wasn't like her to be so offhand. He suspected something more was troubling her.

"Bunny was a good woman, who didn't deserve to be treated so underhandedly by the man she'd loved and trusted. The divorce was final less than a week ago. Bunny, and the children, too, need more love and help than I could give them. To answer your question, no, I don't object to marrying a woman with children."

Lesley was silent after that for a long time. "My dad left us," she said in a small, quiet voice.

Chase carefully chose his words, not knowing how to comment or if he should. "It must have been very painful."

"I was only six and we were going to Disneyland. Mom had worked a second job in order to save extra money for the trip. Dad took the money when he left."

"Oh, Lesley, I'm sorry."

The look in her eyes became distant, as if she were that six-year-old child, reliving the nightmare of being abandoned by her father all over again.

"I know I was wrong to blame myself. I didn't drive my father away, but for years I was convinced if I'd been the son he wanted, he'd never have left."

"Have you had any contact with him since?"

"He called when I was fifteen and wanted to see me."

"Did you?"

She nodded. "After being so bitterly hurt, I didn't put a lot of hope into our meeting. It's funny the things a child will remember about someone. I always thought of my dad as big and strong and invincible. When we met again nine years later, I realized he was weak and selfish. We had lunch together and he told me I could order anything I wanted. I remember I asked for the most expensive thing on the menu even though I didn't like steak. I barely touched the steak sandwich and took it home for the dog. I made sure he knew he paid top dollar to feed our collie, too."

"What prompted him to contact you after all those years?"

Lesley sighed and smiled weakly. "He seemed to want me to absolve him from his guilt. He told me how hard his life had been when he was married to my mother and had all the worries and responsibilities of a family. He claimed he'd married too young, that they'd both made mistakes. He said he couldn't handle the pressures of constantly being in debt and never having the money to do the kind of things he wanted to do.

"That was when I learned the truth. My dad walked out on my mother and me because he wanted to race sports cars. Imagine, driving a sports car meaning more to him than his wife and daughter.

"You might think badly of me, but I wouldn't give him the forgiveness he was seeking—not then. It wasn't until later, in my early twenties, when I learned he'd died of cancer, that I was able to find it in my heart to forgive him.''

''I don't know how any fifteen-year-old could have forgiven someone who'd wounded them so deeply,'' Chase said, reaching for her hand. She gripped his fingers with surprising strength and intuitively Chase knew she didn't often share this painful part of her childhood.

She offered him a small smile and reached for her drink.

''Did your mother ever remarry?''

''Yes,'' Lesley answered, ''to a wonderful man who's perfect for her. You'd have to meet my mother to understand. She has a tendency to be something of a curmudgeon. It took her a long time to find the courage to commit herself to another relationship.

''I was out of high school before she agreed to marry Ken, although they'd dated for years. She never told me this, but my guess is that Ken said either they marry or it was over. I don't think he'd have followed through on the threat, but it worked.

''He and Mom are both retired. They live on a ranch in Montana now and really love it.''

''They sound happy.''

''They'd like a couple of grandkids to spoil someday but—'' Lesley stopped abruptly and her face turned a soft shade of pink.

''But what?'' he inquired.

''Oh, nothing.'' She shrugged, looking decidedly uncomfortable. ''It's just something Daisy said to me this afternoon. By heavens, she might be right.'' Her voice thinned and faded.

''Right about what?''

''Nothing,'' she said quickly.

Whatever the subject, it was apparent Lesley wasn't going to discuss it with him.

"Will you be meeting more women tomorrow?" Lesley asked.

Chase nodded with little enthusiasm. "I should never have agreed to that news story. The phones have been ringing off the hook ever since. There's no way on God's green earth that I could possibly interview eight hundred women in two weeks' time."

"Eight hundred!"

Lesley sounded as shocked as he'd been when he heard the original number of five hundred. Since the story had aired on the noon news, Chase learned three hundred additional calls had poured in.

"That's incredible."

"Just remember, I haven't met a single one I like better than you."

Lesley laughed. "You've already heard my answer to that."

"I don't have much time in Seattle, Lesley. Less than three weeks. I'm going to need to make some decisions soon. If you'd be willing to marry me, I'd promise to be a good husband to you."

"Hold it, fellow," she said raising both hands. "Back up. I'm not in the market for a husband. Not now and possibly never again. Men have played some real tricks on my heart, starting with my father and most recently with Tony. I don't need a man in my life."

"True, but do you want one?"

She hesitated. "I don't know."

"It's something to think about, then, don't you think?"

"Not right now," she answered, her voice insistent. "I don't want to consider anything but having fun. That's my goal for this summer. I want to put the past behind me and get on with life in a positive way."

"I do, too," Chase assured her, and it was true, more than he realized.

"I baked cookies this morning," she announced. "It was the first time in months that I've wanted to bake anything."

"I don't suppose you saved any for me?"

Lesley smiled as if she knew something he didn't. "There's an entire cookie jar reserved for you."

Chase couldn't remember the last time he'd tasted home-baked cookies. Possibly years. "This calls for a picnic, don't you think?"

"Paradise."

He frowned. "Do I have to wait that long to sample those cookies of yours?"

"No, silly. Paradise is in the national park on Mount Rainier. There's a lodge there and several trails and fields of wildflowers so abundant, they'll take your breath away."

"Sounds like Alaska."

"It's one of my favorite places in all the world."

"Let's go, then, first thing in the morning."

"You can't," she said, with that superior look women sometimes get. The one that irritates the hell out of men.

"Why can't I?"

"Because you'll be interviewing a prospective wife. Eight hundred prospective wives to be exact."

Chase cursed under his breath and Lesley burst out laughing. Only then did Chase find any amusement in his predicament. What she didn't seem to understand, and what he was going to have to prove, was that he'd willingly leave all eight hundred willing prospects behind in order to spend time with her.

* * *

The sun had barely peeked over the horizon when Chase arrived. Lesley had been up for an hour, packing their lunch and getting everything ready for their day. Her hiking boots and a sweater were in a sack by the door and the picnic basket was loaded and ready for Chase to carry to his rental car.

"'Morning," she greeted.

"'Morning," Chase returned, leaning forward to gently kiss her.

Lesley swore the kiss was instinctive on both their parts. One taken without thought. One given without hesitation.

Their smiles faded and Lesley's lungs emptied of air. It wasn't supposed to happen like this. She was inches, seconds from walking into his arms before she caught herself.

Chase, however, felt no such restraint and reached for her, pulling her toward him. Even with her mind crying no, she waited impatiently for his mouth to claim hers. Waited impatiently for him to collect her waiting heart.

His touch was gentle and sweet as if he were aware of her feelings.

"I love it when you do that," he whispered, kissing her neck.

"Do what?" she asked and breathed deeply again. The sigh felt as if it had come from the soles of her feet, it was so deep.

He groaned. "You just did it again. That deep, womanly sigh, that tells me so much more than you'd ever be willing to say."

"Don't be ridiculous." She tried to ease away from his hold, but Chase would have none of it. His breath was warm and moist against the sensitized skin of her throat.

He ran his tongue down to the very hollow and his fingers loosened the top button of her blouse.

"I . . . I don't think this is a good idea," Lesley murmured as he backed her against the door. He braced his hands on either side of her head as his eyes gazed into hers.

"I don't want you to think. I want you to feel." He kissed her then with the same wicked sweetness that had broken her resolve seconds before. She sighed, the same sigh he'd mentioned earlier, and regretted it immediately. His body's ready response to her soft release of breath was evident.

"Lesley, hell, I don't know what to do." He braced his forehead against hers, and brushed his nose against hers.

"Kiss me again." She bracketed his face with her hands, buried her fingers in the thickness of his hair and directed his lips back to hers.

He buried his tongue in her mouth, demanding a response from her. Lesley gave him one, opening to him, offering him her own tongue in a blazing, roaring battle of wills. By the time they pulled apart, both were panting and breathless.

His hands anchored the fullness of her breasts. "I want to taste you," he whispered and she knew his need was great.

"I . . . don't know if that's a good idea."

He brushed his thumb against the already taut nipple and it beaded hard and firm and started to throb. The wild sensation that rushed through Lesley was so strong that for a moment she couldn't catch her breath.

For a moment neither of them said anything. Then with trembling fingers, Chase refastened her top shirt button. "I think you might be right," he said with heavy reluctance. "This isn't such a good idea after all. One

taste of you would never be enough. I'm greedy, Lesley.
I want it all. It's better not to start what we can't finish.''

He kissed her gently then, reached for the picnic basket and carried it outside. Lesley was left shaken to the
core. She wouldn't have believed it was possible for any
man to evoke such a violent, heated response from her
with a few kisses.

Her knees were weak as she reached for her boots,
sweater and purse and followed him out the front door.
Chase took her things and stored them beside the picnic
basket in the back of the vehicle. He helped her into the
passenger seat and joined her in the car a moment later,
waiting until she had the seat belt adjusted before he
started the engine.

Neither of them seemed to have much to say on the
long drive to Paradise. Lesley thought to play the role of
tour guide as she had previously, pointing out interesting facts along the way, but changed her mind. She didn't
mention that Mount Rainier National Park was one of
the first parks established in 1899, but it wasn't important that he know that, not if it meant disturbing the
peaceful silence they shared.

Lesley loved Mount Rainier and the way it stood guard
over the Pacific Northwest. The view of the mountain
from Seattle was often breathtaking. Her appreciation
increased even more when she saw the look in Chase's
eyes as they drove the twisting road through the forest-
thick area. He surprised her with his knowledge of trees.

''Everyone recognizes a Douglas fir when they see one,
don't they?'' he teased.

''No.''

They stopped at a campsite and took a break. When
Lesley finished using the facilities, she found Chase
wandering through the mossy, fern-draped valley. Si-

lently she joined him, feeling a closeness and solemnity with Chase, as though they were standing on holy ground. The trees surrounding them were tall and massive, the forest thick and a lush green. Lesley felt a fullness of beauty standing there with Chase. The air was sharp, clean and vibrant.

Chase reached for her hand and entwined his fingers with hers. "Are you ready?" he asked.

Lesley nodded, uncertain exactly what she was agreeing to, and for once in her life not caring.

They got back into the car and traveled the rest of the way until they reached Paradise. Since they hadn't eaten breakfast, Chase suggested they dine in the lodge, which they did.

Afterward, Lesley put her boots on and they walked the trails through the open, subalpine meadowlands, which were shedding their cold blankets of snow.

"You know what I love most here? The flowers, their color, the way they fight their way through the cold and stand tall and proud against the hillside as if to say they'd really accomplished something important," Lesley said as they traipsed up the steep path.

"The flowers respond the way most of us do, don't you think?" Chase asked.

"How's that?"

"With a rich appreciation for life. I feel it here and you do, too. It's like standing on a boulder and looking out over the world and saying, 'Look at me, I've done it.'"

"And what exactly have you done, Chase Goodman?"

He chuckled. "I haven't figured it out yet, but this good feeling is too fantastic to waste."

"I couldn't agree with you more."

They hiked for a couple of hours, the challenge gentle and undemanding as they ascended as far as the tree line. The beauty was unending, spilling out before them like an Impressionistic painting, in vibrant hues of purple, rose and white.

After their hike, they explored the visitor center, then reluctantly headed back to the car.

Lesley was exhausted. The day had been full and exciting, filled with wonder. Over the years, she'd visited Paradise countless times and had always enjoyed herself, but not the way she had this day with Chase. With him, she experienced a spiritual wonder, a spiritual joy, a connecting with nature. A oneness. She could think of no logical way to explain it, any more than she knew why his kisses affected her so strongly.

When they arrived back in Seattle, Eric and Kevin, Daisy's two boys, raced to the car to greet them.

"Hi, Lesley," Eric, the oldest boy greeted, eyeing Chase.

"Hello, boys. This is Chase."

Chase stuck out his hand and cordially shook hands with the youngsters. "Howdy, boys."

"You're sure big. Even bigger than Lesley."

Lesley wasn't sure if that was a compliment or not and let it slide.

"We came to see if you had any more cookies left."

"Mom said you might have some more," Kevin chimed in.

"A few, I think."

"But she made them for me," Chase insisted. "You fellows should make sure I'm willing to share the loot first before asking Lesley."

"She used to make them for us. So we've got first claim."

"You gonna share or not?" Kevin asked, hands on his hips as if to suggest a showdown if it came to that.

Chase rubbed the side of his jaw as if giving the matter heavy consideration.

"Those boys troubling you?" Daisy shouted from the front porch.

"We just want our fair share of Lesley's cookies before Chase eats 'em all."

"I'll buy you cookies," Daisy promised, casting an apologetic look toward Lesley. For her part, Lesley was enjoying this small exchange, especially the way Chase interacted with the two youngsters. Tony had considered Daisy's sons pests and shooed them away whenever they were around. Although he worked with children, he had little rapport with them outside of the classroom.

"We don't want any store-bought cookies," Eric argued.

"Don't try and bake any, either, Mom, not after last time." He looked to Lesley, and whispered, "Even the dog wouldn't eat them."

Lesley smothered a giggle.

"Will you or won't you share the cookies?" Eric demanded of Chase.

Chase himself was having trouble not smiling, Lesley noticed. "I guess I don't have much choice. You two have a prior claim and any judge in the land would take that into account."

"Does that mean he will or he won't?" Kevin asked his brother from the side of his mouth.

"He will," Eric answered, speaking in a whisper. "I think."

"But only if you help us unload the car," Chase insisted, giving them both a few items to haul into the house.

Lesley emptied the cookie jar, setting aside a handful for Chase, and gave the boys their well-earned reward. While Chase was dealing with the picnic basket and the boys, she absently pushed the button for her answering machine, to play back the messages.

"Lesley, it's Tony. I've been doing a lot of thinking lately and thought we should get together to talk. April's out of town this week visiting her mother, so give me a call as soon as you can."

Lesley felt as if she'd been hit in the solar plexus. Instinctively her hands went to her abdomen and she stood frozen for a wild moment in a desperate effort to catch her breath.

She then slowly turned around, not knowing what to do, and discovered Chase standing there, as solid as an oak tree, staring at the answering machine.

Chapter Five

"Well," Chase said, studying Lesley closely. "Are you going to call him?"

"No."

"You're sure?"

He seemed to doubt Lesley and that irritated her, possibly because it was true. A part of her hungered to speak to Tony. School had been out for several weeks now and she was starved for the sight of him. Admitting her weakness, even to herself, demanded rigorous, painful honesty. Tony was married and it sickened her that she would feel this way.

"I'm sure," she snapped, then added, "although it's none of your affair."

He nodded, conceding the issue, his eyes guarded as though he wanted to believe her but wasn't sure he should. "Are you going to invite me in for a cup of coffee?"

Lesley stared at him, not knowing what to say. She needed time alone in order to analyze her feelings, but in the same breath, she didn't want Chase to leave, because once he did, she'd be left to confront her weakness for Tony.

Eric came inside the kitchen, munching loudly on a cookie. "I swear, Lesley's the best cook I ever met," he announced, looking proud to be her neighbor. His jeans had large rips in the knees and his T-shirt was badly stained, but his cheerful countenance was infectious.

"A better cook than Mom," Kevin agreed, rubbing his forearm over his mouth to displace any evidence of crumbs.

"Even Dr. Seuss is a better cook than Mom. Remember the time she made us green eggs and ham for breakfast?" Both boys laughed, and reached for another cookie.

"Say, have you two ever been fishing?" Chase asked unexpectedly.

"Nope." They stared up at Chase with wide, eager eyes.

"I was thinking of asking Lesley to go fishing tomorrow and thought it might be fun if you two came along. You think you could talk your mother into letting you join us?"

"I'll ask," Eric announced, racing from the kitchen.

"I want to ask," Kevin shouted, running after his brother.

Lesley assembled a pot of coffee. She wasn't gullible; she knew exactly why Chase had involved the boys. He wanted to see her again and knew she wouldn't refuse him if it meant disappointing her ragamuffin neighbors. She said as much when she delivered the two mugs of steaming coffee to the table.

"What would you do if I said I couldn't go with you?" she asked, sitting across her round kitchen table from him.

The healing calm she'd experienced earlier with Chase on Mount Rainier had been shattered by Tony's call. She hadn't realized how frail the newfound peace had been nor how easily it would be destroyed. It troubled her that Tony would continue to wield such power over her, especially when she felt she'd made great strides in letting go of her love for him.

"The boys and I'd miss you," Chase said after a moment, "but I'd never disappoint those two. Every boy should go fishing at some point in his life. I'd enjoy it if you could come, but I'll understand if you'd prefer to stay home." He sipped from his coffee and seemed to be waiting for a response from her.

"Would it be all right if I let you know in the morning?"

"Of course."

The front door flew open and Eric and Kevin shot into the room like bullets, breathless with excitement. "Mom said we could go. But she needs to know how much money we need and what we should bring."

"Tell her you don't need a dime and all you have to bring is an extra set of clothes."

"What time?"

"Six sounds good."

"In the morning?" Kevin's eyes rounded with dismay. "We don't usually get up before nine."

"You want to catch trout, don't you?"

"Sure, but..."

"We'll be ready," Eric said, elbowing his brother in the ribs. "Isn't that right, Kevin?"

"Ow. Yeah, we'll be ready."

"Good. Then I'll see you boys bright and early tomorrow morning." Chase ushered the two to the door, while Lesley sat at the table, hiding her amusement.

When Chase returned, he surprised her by taking one last sip of his coffee and carrying the mug to her sink. He returned to the table, placed his hand gently on her shoulder and kissed her cheek. "I'll talk to you later."

"You're leaving?" Suddenly it became vital that he stay because once he left, she feared the temptation to return Tony's call would be too strong to control, too easy to rationalize. Standing abruptly, she wound her arms around her stomach and stared up at him, struggling within herself.

"You don't want me to go?"

She shrugged, unwilling to admit the truth. "I...want you to help me understand why Tony would phone me out of the blue like this. I want you to help me figure out what I should do, but more important, I need you to remind me how wrong it would be to contact him. I can't— won't—betray my own principles."

"Sorry," Chase said softly, sounding genuinely regretful. "Those are things you've got to figure out on your own."

"But..." A thousand protests flooded her mind.

"I'll give you a call in the morning."

"Aren't you going to kiss me?"

He hesitated and desire etched itself across his face. "I'd like nothing better, but I don't think I should."

"Why not?" She moved closer, so close that she could feel his breath against her face, so close that all she need do was ease forward and her lips would meet his.

"I don't think it'd be a good idea, just now." His words were low and troubled.

"I need you to kiss me," she whispered, easing forward just enough so her breasts grazed his chest. She pressed her palms against his shirt and waited.

"I wish..." she continued.

His breathing was erratic, she noted, but no more so than her own.

"What do you wish?" His mouth wandered to her neck and she sighed at the feel of his lips against her skin. She angled her head back, granting him access to every part of her throat, exposing herself to him, revealing her eagerness for his touch.

"You already know what I want," she whispered.

He planted slow kisses to her throat, pausing to moisten the hollow with the tip of his tongue. Shivers of awareness rippled down her arms.

Her mouth sought his and he kissed her, his lips soft and undemanding, his breath like a vapor against her mouth. She slipped her arms around his neck and nestled into his arms, needing the security of his touch to ground her in reality.

He kissed her again and she moaned, lifting her hand to the back of his head and urging him nearer. He kissed her the way a woman dreams a man will kiss her. Hard and impatiently, his need as great as her own. Then he kissed her slowly and thoroughly, teasing her with his tongue, wickedly tracing the outside of her mouth, baiting her until she used her body to beg for more.

He claimed her mouth again and Lesley realized she was obsessed with his kiss as she never had been with Tony's or any other man's. Whether he realized it or not, Chase had kissing down to an art form.

He knew her mood and gauged his kisses accordingly. When she needed to be comforted, he kissed her chastely, reassuringly, until she was ready and eager for more. It was then and only then that he involved his tongue, probing her mouth, brazenly filling her until fiery fingers of need spread through her and her control slipped away.

Lesley moaned deep in her throat and Chase's name fell unevenly from her lips.

Chase lifted his head and kissed her brow. "A man could get accustomed to having a woman say his name like that."

"Oh." It sounded utterly inane, but conversation was beyond her at the moment.

"Marry me, Lesley."

She risked a glance at his face and felt emotion well up in her throat, making speech impossible. Blinking rapidly, she managed to hold the tears at bay.

"All right," he whispered. "We'll do this your way, in increments. Will you join the boys and me in the morning?"

Lesley nodded.

"I was hoping you would." He kissed the tip of her nose. "I have to leave now. Trust me, I'd much rather stay, but I can't and we both know why."

Lesley did know.

It wasn't fair for her to use Chase this way, as a shield against Tony. It was cowardly of her and although she was aware of what she was doing, she still wanted him, still needed him. She would have to stand alone, make her own decisions, and Chase understood that better than she had herself.

"I'll see you bright and early in the morning," he whispered, and released her. As if that was much too long for him to wait to kiss her again, he lowered his mouth to hers once more, kissed her longingly, then exhaled slowly and turned away.

The sound of the front door closing followed seconds later, and Lesley stood in the middle of her kitchen with the phone just inches away.

"A trout can sure put up a big fight," Eric announced with a self-satisfied look in his brother's direction after he caught his first fish.

The four of them stood on the banks of Green River, their lines dangling in a pool of deep water. By luck of the draw, Eric had managed to catch the first trout. While Chase helped the boy remove the squirming fish from the line and rebait his hook, Lesley whispered reassurances to Kevin.

"Don't worry, you'll snag one, too."

"But what if I don't?" Kevin asked, hanging his head so low his chin rested against his chest. "Eric always gets everything first just because he's older. It isn't fair. It just isn't fair."

No sooner were the words out of his mouth when his line dipped with such force that he nearly lost his fishing rod. His triumphant gaze flew to Lesley and he smiled as if he had the world on a string. "I've got one!"

Chase immediately diverted his attention to the younger of the two boys, coaxing him as he had Eric earlier, tutoring him until the boy had reeled in the trout and Chase was able to remove the good-size fish from the hook.

"Is mine bigger than Eric's?" Kevin demanded.

"You'll have to check that for yourself."

"Mine's bigger," Kevin announced a moment later with a smug look.

Lesley found the younger boy's conviction amusing, but said nothing. To prove his point, Kevin held up both fish and asked Lesley to judge, but it was impossible when one of the trout was squirming and wiggling on the end of Kevin's finger.

They spent the better part of the morning fishing, until both boys had reached their limit. Although Chase had brought Lesley a fishing rod, she didn't do much fishing herself. Twice she got a fish on the line, but both times she let the boys reel them in for her. Chase did the same, letting the boys experience the thrill.

By eleven o'clock, all four were famished.

"Let's have trout for lunch," Chase suggested.

"I thought Lesley made us sandwiches," Kevin stated, eyeing the fish suspiciously. "I don't much care for fish, unless it's fish and chips, and then I'll eat it."

"That's because you've never had anyone cook trout the way the Indians do." Chase explained a method of slow cooking, wrapping the fish in leaves and mud and then burying them in the coals that had even Lesley's mouth watering in anticipation. He also explained the importance of never allowing the fish they'd caught to go to waste. Both boys nodded solemnly as if they'd accepted the wisdom of his words. By then, Lesley guessed, both boys thought Chase walked on water.

"I'm going to need your help," he said, instructing the boys to gather kindling for the fire. "Then you can help me clean the trout."

"You won't need me for this, will you?" Lesley asked hopefully.

"Women are afraid of guts," Eric explained for Chase's benefit.

"Is that so?"

"They go all weird over that kind of stuff. Mom's the same way. One time, the neighbor's cat, a black one named Midnight . . . you know Midnight, don't you, Lesley?"

She nodded.

"Midnight brought a dead bird into the yard and Mom started going all weird and yelling. We thought someone was trying to murder her."

"I thought Dad was back," Eric inserted, and Chase's gaze connected briefly with Lesley's and for an instant fire leapt into his eyes.

"Anyway, Mom asked Kevin and me to bury it. I don't think she's ever forgiven Midnight, either. She gives him mean looks whenever he comes to visit and shoos him away."

"I think that dead bird's the reason she let us get Spot. She knew Midnight wasn't going to be bringing her any more gifts with a big dog around."

While the boys were discussing a woman's aversion to the sight of blood, Lesley brought out the plastic tablecloth and spread it over the picnic table close to where they'd parked the car.

"That's another thing," Eric said, knowingly, motioning his head toward her. "A woman wants to make everything fancy. Real men don't eat on a tablecloth. Kevin and I never would if it wasn't for Mom and Lesley."

"Don't forget Grandma," Kevin said.

"Right, and Grandma, too."

"Those feminine touches to a meal can be nice, though," Chase told the boys. "I live in a big log cabin up in Alaska and it gets mighty lonesome during the winters. Last January I would have done just about anything to have a pretty face smile across the dinner table from me even if it did mean having to eat on a tablecloth. I wouldn't have cared if she'd spread out ten of them. It would have been a small price to pay for her company."

"You mean you *wanted* a woman with you?" Eric sounded surprised.

"Men like having women around?" Kevin asked.

"Of course," Chase returned casually.

"My dad doesn't feel that way. He said he was glad to be rid of us. He said lots of mean things that made Mom cry and he hit her sometimes, too."

Chase crouched down before Eric and Kevin and talked to them for several moments. She wasn't able to hear everything he said, making trips back and forth to the car the way she was, but she knew whatever it was had a solid impact on the boys. She was touched when the three of them hugged.

After a while the fire Chase had built had burned down to hot coals. The boys and Chase wrapped the cleaned fish in a bed of leaves and packed them in mud before burying them in the dirt, covering the thin layer with the hot coals.

"While we're waiting," Chase suggested, "we'll sample those sandwiches Lesley packed and go exploring."

"Great." After collecting their sandwiches, both boys were eager and shot off into the distance, forging ahead like a pair of Indian scouts. Lesley gratefully offered excuses to stay behind. Trekking into the woods, chasing after those two, was beyond her. She brought out a lounge chair she'd packed, spread it out and gratefully sank into it.

She must have dozed off because she woke with both boys staring down at her, studying her as if she were a specimen under a microscope.

"She's awake," Eric cried.

"Let's eat," Kevin said eagerly. "I'm starved."

Lesley had the plates and plastic silverware set out on the table, along with a bag of potato chips, veggies and a cake she'd baked the night before.

Chase dug up the fish, scraped aside the dried mud and peeled back the leaves. The tantalizing aroma of the trout took Lesley by surprise. Until then she hadn't realized how hungry she was.

They ate until they were stuffed, until they couldn't down another morsel. Chase and the boys conscientiously dealt with the garbage and loaded up the vehicle, after Lesley had packed the leftovers—not that there were many.

Eric and Kevin fell asleep in the back seat on the ride home.

"They really enjoyed themselves," Lesley whispered. "They'll remember this day all their lives. It was very sweet of you to invite them along."

She watched as his gaze briefly moved to his rearview mirror as he glanced at the boys. "I'd like to meet their father in a dark alley someday. I have no tolerance for a man who hits a woman."

"He has a drinking problem," Lesley explained.

"Is that an excuse?"

"No, just an explanation."

"The man should be punished for telling his sons he was glad to be rid of them. What kind of father would say such a thing?"

He didn't seem to expect an answer, which was just as well since Lesley didn't have one to give him.

Daisy was back from her computer classes by the time they arrived. The boys stirred awake when Chase cut the engine. As soon as they realized they were home, they darted out of the car and into the house, eager to tell their mother of their adventures.

Daisy came out of the house with her sons and instructed them to help unload the car for Lesley, which they did willingly.

Lesley had been neighbors and friends with Daisy for three years. She'd watched this no-nonsense woman make some hard decisions in that time, but never once had she seen her friend cry. But there were tears in Daisy's eyes now.

"Thank you," she whispered to Chase.

"No problem. I was happy to have them with us. You're raising two fine boys there, Daisy. You should be proud of them."

"Oh, damn," she whispered, holding an index finger under each eye. "You're going to have me bawling here in a minute. I just wanted to thank you both."

"Daisy?" Lesley asked gently. "Is everything all right?"

"Of course everything's all right. A woman can shed a few tears every now and again, can't she?"

"Sure, but..."

"I know. I'm making a fool of myself. It's just that I appreciate what you did for my boys. I've never seen them so excited and so happy." Lesley wasn't expecting to be hugged, but Daisy reached for her, nearly squeezing the breath from her lungs with the force of her embrace. "I just wanted to thank you for being my friend," she murmured, wiped her hand under her nose and returned to her house.

Eric and Kevin were off, eager to relate their escapades to their neighborhood friends.

Chase followed Lesley into the kitchen. He helped her unload the picnic basket then stopped abruptly, looking over at her.

"Is something the matter?" she asked.

"It looks like you've got a call on your answering machine."

Lesley's heart felt frozen in her chest. Trying to be nonchalant about it, she walked over to the device and pushed the playback button. This time, Tony's voice didn't rip through her like the serrated blade of a knife. It felt anticlimactic to hear him again so soon.

"Lesley, it's Tony. When you didn't return my call, I stopped by the house. You weren't home. I need to talk to you. Call me soon. Please."

Lesley looked at Chase, wishing she were able to read his thoughts, wishing she could gauge her own. His eyes were darker than she could ever remember seeing them and his jaw was stiff.

"Are you going to contact him?"

She wasn't any more confident this time than she had been earlier. "I don't know."

"I see."

"You want to remind me he's a married man, don't you?" she cried. "I know that, Chase. I don't know why he's calling and I don't know what he wants from me."

"Get real, Lesley. You know exactly what he wants. Didn't he as much as say April was out of town?"

"Tony's not like that." Again, she didn't know why she felt the need to defend him. She had so often that it came naturally to her, she guessed. Although, it did seem obvious to Lesley then that Tony might be unfaithful to April, as he had been to her.

"You know him better than I do," Chase admitted grudgingly. "I've got to get back," he announced stiffly, as though he couldn't get away from her fast enough.

"Are you interviewing more...applicants?" she asked him on the way to the door, making conversation, not wanting their fun day to end on a sour note.

"Yes," he said briskly. "Several as a matter of fact."

His answer surprised her. "When?"

"I talked to some last night and I have more scheduled for later this afternoon and evening."

"You'll call me?" she asked, trailing him. Her gaze refused to leave his chest. Chase Goodman had one of the finest chests she'd ever had the good fortune to view in a man. It was a chest she very much wanted to be pressed against. A chest she very much wanted to touch without the barrier of a shirt.

He hesitated, not looking at her. An eternity passed before he nodded. "All right." It seemed to demand a good deal for him to agree to something so small.

Lesley longed to reassure him; that was what Chase was looking for her to do. To promise him she wouldn't contact Tony. But Lesley couldn't do that—not this time. She remembered what he'd told her, about being a sore loser when it came to a woman. What Chase didn't understand was that she would never try to manipulate one man against another, especially him against Tony.

"I'll look forward to hearing from you," she said, standing on the other side of the screen door, watching him walk away from her. She had the craziest feeling he was taking a piece of her heart with him.

She waited until his car was out of view before she breathed again. It wasn't possible to know a man for so short a while and adequately judge her feelings. She was attracted to him, but any other red-blooded woman with two eyes in her head would be, too. His chest wasn't the only desirable attribute to this man.

Then there was Tony. She'd loved him for so long that she didn't know how to stop. He'd been a vital part of her life and without him her world felt empty and meaningless.

Lesley walked back into her kitchen and listened to the message on her answering machine once more. She thought about phoning Lori and asking for advice, but decided against it. Her friend had claimed she'd be getting back to her later in the week, and hadn't.

Daisy was the more logical choice, although her feelings toward Tony were well-known. Lesley found her neighbor wearing an itsy bitsy bikini, soaking up the sun on a chaise longue while propping an aluminum shield under her chin. Amused, Lesley walked over to the picket fence and studied her wacky neighbor.

"Where in heaven's name did you get that?" Lesley asked, not bothering to hide her amusement.

"Don't get excited. It's one of those microwave pizza boxes the boys like so well, with those fancy silver linings. I figured I'd put it to good use now that they're finished with the pizza."

"Honestly, girl, you crack me up."

"I've only got so much time a day to get any sun. I've got to make the most of it while I can."

"I know, I know."

"Where'd Chase take off to?"

Lesley looked away. Eric and Kevin were riding their bikes down the sidewalk. They saw her and waved.

"He had to get back to his hotel. Did I tell you eight hundred women had responded to his billboard?"

Daisy's knees were raised and her eyes closed. "It seems to me that it's a shame you're not one of them. What's the matter, Lesley, is it beneath your dignity?"

"Yes," she answered abruptly.

Daisy's sigh revealed how exasperated her neighbor had become with her. "That's a shame, sweetie, because that man's worth ten Tonys. Hands down."

Lesley's fingers closed around the two pickets of the fence. "It's funny that you should mention Tony because he's been calling me."

"What does that poor excuse of a man have to say for himself?"

"He claims he needs to talk to me."

"I'll just bet."

"He left two messages on my machine and Chase was here both times when I played them back."

Daisy sighed. "Chase isn't the type to stand still for that nonsense. Did he set you straight?"

"Daisy! I wouldn't have listened had he tried. I don't need a man to tell me what to do and I resent you even suggesting such a thing."

"You're right, of course. Which one of us truly needs a man? I don't and you've proved you don't, either. But you know having one around can be a real comfort at times."

"I don't know what I'm going to do," Lesley whispered, worrying her lower lip.

"About Chase and all those women?"

It amazed her the way Daisy always brought the conversation back to Chase. "No, about Tony calling me."

"You've been miserable because that slimeball dumped you," Daisy continued with barely a pause. "I find it ironic that when you meet up with a really decent guy, Tony would come sniffin' around. Does this guy have radar or what?"

Lesley smiled. "I doubt it."

"He couldn't tolerate the thought of you with another man, you know."

"Don't be ridiculous. He didn't want me, Daisy. You seem to be forgetting that."

"Of course he wants you. It's a matter of pride to him to keep two women in love with him. Don't kid yourself. His ego eats it up."

"He's married."

Daisy snorted. "When has that ever stopped a man?"

"I'm sure you're wrong." Here she was defending him when she hadn't a clue what he wanted from her.

"Listen, sweetie, you might have a fancy college degree but when it comes to knowing men, you're as naive as they come. Why do you think Tony didn't want you transferring to another school? He wants to keep his eye on you. Trust me, the minute you reveal the least amount of interest in another man, he'll be there like stink on—"

"I get the picture, Daisy."

"Fine, but do you get the message?"

Lesley gnawed at her lip. "I think so."

Daisy hesitated a moment and lowered the aluminum shield. She turned her head to look at Lesley. "You're afraid, aren't you? Afraid of what will happen if you do call Tony back."

Lesley nodded.

"Are you still in love with that rat?"

Once more she nodded.

"Oh, Lesley, you dope. You don't need that bum, not when you've got someone like Chase. He's crazy about you, but he isn't stupid. He's not going to butt his head against a brick wall, and who would blame him? Not me."

"I barely know Chase."

"What more do you need to know?"

"Daisy, he's looking for a wife."

"So what?" Her neighbor pressed impatiently.

"I'm not in love with Chase."

"Do you like him?"

"Of course I do. Otherwise I wouldn't continue to see him."

"What are you expecting, sweetie? This guy is manna from heaven. If you want to spend the rest of your life mooning over Tony, feel free. As far as I'm concerned, that man's going to do his best to make you miserable for as long as he can."

"Chase's from Alaska," Lesley argued.

"So? You don't have any family here. There's nothing holding you back, other than Tony, is there? Is a married man worth all that grief, Lesley?"

"No." How small her voice sounded, how uncertain.

"Do you want to lose Chase?"

"I don't know..."

"You don't know? Sometimes I want to clobber you, Lesley. I can't think of where you'd ever find another man as good as Chase Goodman, but if that doesn't concern you, then far be it for me to point out the obvious." She swung her legs from the chaise longue. "If you want my advice, I'd say go for it and marry the guy. I sincerely doubt that you'll ever be sorry."

Lesley wished she could be as sure of that, but she wasn't. She wasn't even sure how she was going to get through another night without calling Tony.

Chapter Six

Chase rubbed his hand over his face and forced himself to relax. He wasn't being fair to the women he'd interviewed. He tried, heaven knew he'd tried to concentrate on what they'd said, but it hadn't worked, not in a single incidence.

He'd ask a question, listen intently for the first moment or two, and then his mind would start to drift. What irritated him most was the subject that dominated his thoughts so completely.

Lesley.

She was in love with that bastard Tony, although she was struggling to hide it. Not from him, but herself. The signs were there like graffiti sprayed against a freshly painted wall.

If he had more time, he might have a chance with Lesley. But he didn't. Even if he could afford a couple of months or more to court and woo her, he wasn't sure it would be enough.

The best thing, the only thing, he could do was accept that she was lost to him, cut his losses and do what he could to make up for wasted time.

"That's the last of them for this evening," Sandra, his secretary said, letting herself into the room. The door clicked softly from behind her.

"Good." He was exhausted to the bone.

"I've got appointments starting first thing tomorrow morning. Are you sure you're up to much more of this?"

He nodded, although he wasn't the least bit confident of anything. The faces and stories had begun to blend together until they all started to look and sound the same.

Sandra hesitated. "Has anyone caught your fancy yet?"

Chase chuckled, not because he found her question amusing, but because he was susceptible to one of the most basic human flaws—wanting what he couldn't have. He wanted Lesley. "The woman I'd like to marry is in love with someone else and won't marry me."

"Isn't that the way it generally works?" Sandra offered sympathetically.

"It must," he whispered, stretching out his legs and crossing them at the ankles. He wasn't accustomed to so much sitting and was getting restless and weary. The city was beginning to wear on him and the thought of his cabin on the tundra gained appeal by the minute.

"Is there one woman that's stuck out in your mind?" He motioned for Sandra to sit down and she did, taking the chair across from him.

"A couple," the receptionist admitted. "Do you remember Anna Lincoln and LaDonna Ransom?"

Chase didn't. "Describe them to me."

"LaDonna's that petite blonde you saw yesterday evening, the one that's working in the King County Assessor's office."

For the life of him, Chase couldn't recall the woman, not when there'd been so many. There'd been several blondes, and countless faces and little that made one stand out in his mind over another.

"But I hesitate to recommend her. She's a fragile thing, and I don't know how well she'd adjust to winters that far north. Seattle's climate is temperate and nothing like what you experience. But she was sweet and I think you'd grow to love her, given the opportunity."

"What about Anna Lincoln?"

"We chatted for a bit before the interview and she seemed to be such a nice girl. Ambitious, too. Of course there was the one drawback," Sandra hesitated. "She's really not very pretty, at least not when you compare her to several of the other women who've applied."

"Beauty doesn't count for much as far as I'm concerned. I'm not exactly a movie star myself, you know."

Sandra must have felt obliged to argue with him because she put up something of a fuss contradicting him. By the time she finished, she had him sounding like he should consider running for Mr. Universe. At the same moment, Chase realized he wasn't paying this woman enough.

"At any rate, I liked Anna and I think she'd suit you. If you want I'll get her file."

"Please."

Sandra left and returned a couple of minutes later with the necessary papers. Chase was reading them over when the receptionist bid him good-night. He waved absently as he scanned the details listed. There wasn't a picture enclosed, which might have jogged his memory so he could remember speaking to her. The details she'd written down about herself described at least twenty other women he'd interviewed in the past week.

He set the file aside and relaxed against the back of his chair, wondering if Anna's lips were as soft and pliable as Lesley's, or if she fit in his arms as though she'd been designed with him in mind. Probably not. No use trying to fool himself.

He reread the information and, exhaling sharply with defeat, set aside the file. At the rate things were happening, he would return to Twin Creeks without the bride he'd come to find.

"Lori?" Lesley was so excited to find her friend at home that her voice rose unnaturally high.

"Lesley? Hi."

"Hi yourself. I've been waiting to hear from you. We were going to get together this week, remember?"

"We were? Oh, right, I did say I'd call you, didn't I? It's been so crazy all week. Oh, Les, you'll never guess what happened. Larry asked me to marry him!" She let out a scream that sounded as though she were being strangled.

"Lori!"

"I know, I've got to stop doing that, but every time I think of Larry and me together, I get so thrilled I can barely stand it."

"You haven't been dating him that long, have you?"

"Long enough. I'm crazy about this guy, Lesley, really crazy, and for once in my life I've found a man who feels the same way about me."

"Congratulations." Lesley put as much punch into the word as her fragile heart would allow. She *was* thrilled for Lori, and wished her fellow teacher and Larry every happiness. But in the same breath, in the same heart-beat, she was so jealous she wanted to bury her head in the sand and weep with frustration.

Truth demanded a price and being honest with herself had taken its toll all week with Lesley. First, she'd been forced to admit she continued to love Tony despite her best efforts to put him out of her life. It was hopeless, useless and masochistic. She didn't need Daisy to tell her she was setting herself up for heartache. Not when she could see it herself as plain as anything.

Despite the temptation, she hadn't returned Tony's calls. Her sense of honor hadn't prompted the action nor had her sense of right and wrong.

Good old-fashioned fear was what kept her away from the telephone. Fear of what she'd do if Tony admitted he'd made a mistake and wanted her back in his life. Fear of what she might become if he came to her, claiming he loved her, needed her.

On the heels of this painful insight came the news of Lori's engagement. Now there was just her and Jo Ann, the only two single women left at the school. And Jo Ann didn't count, not technically.

Jo Ann had separated from her husband a year earlier and she'd taken back her maiden name. But recently they'd been talking. It wouldn't surprise Lesley if the two of them decided to make another go of their marriage.

Now Lori was engaged.

"Larry insists on a short engagement, which is fine with me. I'd like it if we could have the wedding before school starts this fall, and he's agreed. You'll be one of my bridesmaids, won't you?"

"I'd be honored." That would make six times now that Lesley had stood up for friends. What was the old saying? Always a bridesmaid and never a bride. It certainly applied in her case.

By fall she'd be returning to the same school, the same classroom, the one directly down from Tony's room. April's class was on the other half of the building. They'd all return, enthusiastic for the new school year, eager to get started after the long break.

Tony would glance her way with that special look in his eyes and she wouldn't be able to glance away from him. He'd know in a heartbeat she loved him, and worse, so would April and everyone else on the staff. That humiliation far outweighed the possibility of her being the only unmarried faculty member.

Lesley didn't know what she was going to do. She should never have allowed Tony to talk her out of transferring to another school. Perhaps she'd asked for another assignment just so he would beg her to stay; she didn't know anymore, didn't trust herself or her motives.

"Larry talked to my dad, and formally asked for my hand in marriage," Lori was saying when Lesley pulled her thoughts back to her friend. "He's so traditional and sweet. It's funny, Les, but when it's right, it's right, and you know it in your gut. It wouldn't have mattered if we'd dated three months or three years."

"Didn't you know Larry before?"

"Briefly. He was a friend of my brother's, but I don't remember ever meeting him until this spring, although he claims we did. He does a good job of pretending to be insulted that I've forgotten."

Lesley smiled. Lori's happiness sang through the wire like a melodious love song, full of joy and spirit. They spoke for a few minutes longer, of getting together with three of Lori's other friends and choosing the dresses, but it was all rather vague.

Jealous. That was what Lesley was. Jealous of one of her best friends. She hated admitting it, but there was no way to discount the hard knot in the pit of her stomach. It wasn't that she wished ill for Lori and Larry. Never that.

Her feelings were wrapped around the scars of her past, of standing alone, helpless and lost. Those deep, dark dreaded feelings of abandonment.

When she finished talking to Lori, Lesley reached for the phone, called a florist friend and had a congratulatory bouquet sent to Lori and Larry with her warmest wishes.

Housework, Lesley decided. That was what a woman did when she suffered from pangs of guilt. It was either that or bury herself in a gallon of gourmet ice cream. She stripped her bed, stuffed the sheets in the washer and was hanging them out on the line when Eric and Kevin found her.

"Is Chase coming over today?" Eric wanted to know.

"He didn't say," she answered as noncommittally as she could, not knowing what to tell the boys. She didn't want to disappoint them, or encourage them, either.

"Can you call him and ask?"

Lesley shoved a clothespin onto a sheet, anchoring the linen to the line. "I don't have his phone number," she realized for the first time.

"He'll be calling you, won't he?"

"I . . . don't know." She'd asked him to and he'd said he would, but that wasn't any guarantee. He'd been annoyed with her when they parted, convinced she would contact Tony despite her shaky reassurances otherwise.

Chase was an intelligent and sensitive man; he knew better than to involve himself in a dead-end relationship. It wouldn't surprise her if he never contacted her again.

The thought struck her hard and fast, like a swift karate chop to the abdomen. The pain it produced surprised her. She hadn't realized how much she'd come to treasure their brief time together.

"What do you mean you don't know if he'll call you again?" Eric demanded. "You have to see him again because Kevin and me wrote him a letter to thank him for taking us fishing."

"Mom made us," Kevin volunteered. His front tooth was missing and Lesley noticed its absence for the first time.

She caught the younger boy by the chin and angled his head toward the light, although he squirmed. "Kevin, you lost your tooth. When did this happen?"

"Last night."

"Congratulations," she said, releasing him. "Did you leave it out for the Tooth Fairy?"

The boy rolled his eyes. "I don't believe in that silly stuff anymore and neither does Eric."

"What do you expect when they've got me for a mother?" Daisy announced, stepping out the back porch, her hands braced against her hips. "I never did believe in feeding kids all that garbage about Santa Claus and the Easter bunny. Life's hard enough without their own mother filling their heads with that kind of nonsense."

"We get gifts and candy and other stuff," Kevin felt obliged to inform Lesley, "but we know who gave them to us. Mom gave me a dollar for the tooth."

"He already spent it, too, on gum and candy."

"I shared, didn't I?"

"Boys, why don't you run along," Daisy advised.

"What about the letter?"

Daisy shrugged. "Give it to Lesley and let her worry about it." With that, her neighbor returned to the house.

What Lesley told the boys about not knowing Chase's phone number was a half-truth. There was always the number on the billboard. If she hadn't heard from him by that evening, she'd leave a message for him through the answering service, although she had serious doubts it would ever reach him.

After a polite knock, Sandra let herself into the suite where Chase was sitting. He'd interviewed ten more women and was scheduled to meet with another fifteen later in the day.

He hadn't talked to or seen Lesley in two days and the temptation to call her or even hop in his car and go see her was gaining momentum every hour. He was trying, really trying, to meet a woman he liked as well as Lesley. Thus far he hadn't succeeded. Hadn't come anywhere close to succeeding.

"Does the name Lesley Campbell mean anything to you?" Sandra asked unexpectedly.

Chase straightened as a chill shot through his blood. "Yes, why?"

"She left a message with the answering service. Apparently she went to a good deal of trouble to explain that she wasn't responding to the billboard you rented. She wanted it understood that the two of you knew one another previously."

"She left a message?"

"Yes." Sandra handed him the pink slip. "I thought it might be a trick. Several of the applicants have tried a variety of methods to get your attention."

Chase didn't need to be reminded of that. Flowers arrived almost daily, along with elaborately wrapped presents. Some of the gifts had shocked him. He hadn't accepted any of the offerings. The floral bouquets he had delivered to a nearby nursing home and the gifts were dispensed with quickly. He left their disposal to Sandra's capable hands.

One woman, a day earlier, had arrived in full winter garb, carrying a long-barreled shotgun as though that would prove she were ready, willing and able to withstand the harsh unforgiving winters of the Arctic. He wasn't sure what the gun was meant to signify. Possibly she intended to hunt down polar bears.

Chase wasn't sure where she'd gotten the outfit. A rental agency, he guessed. She resembled Daniel Boone more than she did a prospective wife. Chase had quickly lost his patience with her and sent her on her merry way.

He glanced down at the pink message slip in his hand and tried to decide what he was going to do. Returning Lesley's call could just be prolonging the inevitable. He wondered if she'd spoken to Tony and what had come of their conversation. The minute he learned she had, it would be over for them. Possibly it was over already.

Objectivity was beyond him at this point. As far as he was concerned, Tony was bad news. All the other man represented for Lesley was heartache and grief. If she wasn't smart enough to figure that out for herself, then he couldn't help her.

It infuriated Chase that Lesley's former fiancé would continue to manipulate her in order to stroke his own vanity. Chase couldn't make himself believe it was for anything else that Tony needed her.

He waited until Sandra had left the room before he reached for the phone and dialed Lesley's number. She answered on the second ring. The sound of her voice produced an empty, achy feeling in the area close to his heart. The pang surprised him; he'd been unaware she had the power to hurt him. He had no one to blame but himself. If Lesley hurt him, it was because he'd allowed it.

"It's Chase."

"Chase..." She sounded breathless and uncertain. "Thank you for returning my call. I wasn't sure you'd get my message."

"How are you?" He never had been a brilliant conversationalist, but he generally was more adept than this.

"Fine. How about you?"

"I've been busy."

"Yeah, me, too."

Silence. Chase didn't know if he should break it or if she should. They hadn't fought, hadn't spoken so much as a cross word to one another. He couldn't even say they'd disagreed, but there was a gap between them that felt as large and as deep as the Grand Canyon.

"Eric and Kevin were asking about you," Lesley said before the silence threatened to crash though the sound barrier. "I wasn't sure what to tell them."

"I see."

"They wrote you a letter and asked me to give it to you."

"That was thoughtful. They're good kids," he said carefully.

The ball was in her court. If she wanted to see him, she was going to have to ask.

"I could mail it."

His back straightened. "Fine." He rattled off his address and was about to make an excuse to get off the line when she spoke again.

"I'd rather you came for it yourself."

Finally. Chase prayed she couldn't hear his sigh of relief. "When?"

"Whenever it's convenient for you." She sounded unsure of herself again, as though she already regretted the invitation.

"If you want, you could leave it on your porch and I could stop off for it sometime."

"No." Her objection came fast enough to lend him hope. "Tomorrow," she suggested. "Or tonight, whichever you prefer."

"I'll have to check my schedule." He didn't know why it was necessary to continue with this silliness but he felt obliged to do so.

"I can wait."

He pressed the receiver to his chest and silently counted to ten, feeling like the biggest fool who'd ever roamed the face of the earth.

"Tonight looks like it would be the best. Say an hour?"

"That would be fine. I'll look for you then."

Chase waited until he heard the click of the receiver before he tossed the phone in the air and deftly caught it with one hand behind his back. "Hot damn," he shouted loud enough to send Sandra barging into the room.

"Is everything all right?"

"Everything, my dear Ms. Zielger, is just peachy." He caught her in his arms and waltzed across the room, planting a fat kiss on her cheek before opening the connecting door that led to his suite.

For the second time, Lesley fluffed up the decorator pillows at the end of her sofa. Holding one to her stomach, she exhaled slowly, praying she was doing the right thing.

The doorbell chimed and she must have leapt a good five inches off the ground. It was early, too early for Chase. She opened the door to find Daisy standing on the other side.

"He's coming?"

"Yes, how'd you know?"

Daisy laughed. "You wouldn't dress up like that for me."

"It's too much isn't it?" She'd carefully gone over her wardrobe, choosing beige silk pants, a cream-colored top and a soft orange blazer. Her silver earrings were crescent shaped and the necklace dangling from her neck was a round gold-edged magnifying glass.

"You look fabulous, darling," Daisy commented in a lazy drawl. "Just fab-u-lous."

"Am I being too obvious?"

"Honey, compared to me, you're extremely subtle. Just be yourself and you'll do fine." She walked around the coffee table and eyed the cheese-and-cracker tray.

"What do you think?"

Daisy shrugged. "It's a nice touch."

"I've got wine cooling in the kitchen. I don't look too eager, do I?"

"No."

"You're sure?" Lesley had never been less certain of anything. Her nerves were shattered, her composure crumbling and her self-confidence was at its lowest ebb.

"There must be something in the air," Daisy said, reaching for a cracker. She was about to dip it in the nut-rolled cheddar cheese ball when Lesley slapped her hand, stopping her.

"That's for Chase," she chastised.

"Didn't you tell me your friend Lori was getting married?"

"Yes."

Daisy relaxed against the sofa cushion and crossed her legs, swinging her foot dangerously close to the cheese roll. "You'll never guess who's been calling."

"Who?"

"Charlie Glenn called and formally asked me out on a date. Charlie and me? He shocked me so bad I said yes without even thinking. It's been so long since someone who wasn't half gassed asked me out that I didn't know what to say."

"I've been saying for weeks that Charlie's sweet on you."

Daisy flopped her wrist at Lesley. "Get outta here."

"I'm serious," Lesley insisted.

"And that's why I think there must be something in the air. First you meet Chase, then Lori and Larry decide to tie the knot and then Charlie asks me out."

Lesley smiled. Since her divorce, Daisy had sworn off men. To the best of Lesley's knowledge, her neighbor hadn't dated in a couple of years. More than once Daisy had insisted it would take one hell of a man to replace no man, and Lesley suspected her friend was right.

"Where's Charlie taking you?"

"Taking us. He included the boys. We're going to Wild Waves. Eric and Kevin are ecstatic. Did you know Charlie's been married before? I didn't, and it came as something of a shock to me. He never mentioned he had a kid, either. You could have blown me over with a feather. Anyway, his son's a couple of years older than Eric and he wants the five of us to get together."

"I think that's sweet."

"Yeah, I guess I do, too, but you know, I'm a little surprised at myself. I'd never thought about Charlie in a romantic way, but I'm beginning to think I might be able to at some point down the road. I'm not rushing into anything, mind you, and neither is he. We've both been burned and neither one of us is willing to walk through fire a second time." Daisy reached for a second cracker. "Here I am jabbering away as though Charlie asked me to marry him or something. It's just a date. I have to keep telling myself that."

"I think Charlie's wonderful."

"He's got a soft spot where his heart's supposed to be."

Lesley recalled how the bartender had given her a stiff drink on the house the night Tony broke their engagement. She'd walked the streets for hours and finally landed in the cocktail lounge where Daisy worked and Charlie tended bar. Because she so rarely drank the hard stuff, one whiskey on the rocks had Lesley three sheets into the wind. Charlie had half carried her to Daisy's car, she remembered. His touch was gentle and his words soothing, although for the life of her she couldn't understand a word he was saying.

"Let me know what happens," Daisy said, uncrossing her long legs and bounding off the sofa. She walked to the door and opened it, then turned around toward Lesley once more. "You're sure you know what you're doing?"

"No," she cried. She wasn't the least bit sure of anything at the moment except the knot in her stomach.

"I'll do my best to keep the boys out of your hair but they're anxious to see Chase again. He certainly made an impression on those two. They think he's the cat's meow," she said with a smile, then walked out.

Lesley didn't blame the boys. Chase had shown the three of them a marvelous time.

The phone pealed and Lesley glared at it accusingly. She let the machine catch the calls most of the time now, not answering the phone when there was a chance the caller could be Tony. It had been pure luck that she'd picked up the receiver when Chase had phoned. Her reaction had been instinctive, without thought. But she was pleased she had answered the call because it had been Chase.

The phone rang a second time and the machine automatically clicked on after the third ring. Whoever was phoning her wasn't willing to listen to the message and disconnected the line.

No sooner had she finished watching the tape circle when the doorbell chimed. It had to be Chase and she breathed in a calming breath, squared her shoulders and crossed the room.

A smile was painted across her face as she opened the door.

"Hello, Lesley."

"Hello," she said, stepping aside for Chase to enter. "Come in, please."

He hadn't taken his eyes off her, which was reassuring and disconcerting both at once.

"I'm pleased you could come."

"Thank you for inviting me."

How stiff they were with one another, like awkward strangers, standing guard over their pride. "Sit down, please," she said, gesturing toward the sofa.

Chase took a seat and eyed the cheese and crackers appreciatively.

"Would you like something to drink?" she asked, rubbing her palms together, although she wasn't the least bit chilled. "I have a bottle of white wine cooling, if you'd care for that. There's a pot of coffee, too, if you'd prefer something hot."

"Wine would be nice."

"I thought so," she said eagerly, smiling. She moved into the kitchen and was surprised when Chase chose to follow her.

"Do you need any help opening the wine?"

"No, I'm fine, thanks." Someone more dainty might have trouble removing a cork, but she was perfectly capable of handling the task. He stood and watched her expertly open the wine. She gave the bottle a couple of moments to breathe, then filled two wineglasses.

"You mentioned the boys' letter," Chase said, jogging her memory. Their thank-you note had been an excuse to contact him and they both knew it.

"I'll get it for you," she said, leaving him briefly while she retrieved the note. "They really are grateful for the time you spent with them."

He read over the note, grinned and handed it to her to read. Eric had written the words, and Kevin had decorated the handmade card with a variety of different colored fish in odd shapes and sizes. Both boys had penned their names.

"So," Lesley said, leading the way back into the living room. "How have you been?"

"Fair." He sat next to her on the sofa. "How about you?"

"Fair." That was a good assessment.

Chase's gaze studied her. "Are you going to tell me what Tony wanted or are you going to make me guess?"

"I don't know," she answered, sipping from her wine. She hoped he didn't detect the slight shake in her hand.

"You don't know if you're going to tell me or if you're going to make me guess?"

She smiled. "No. I don't know what he wanted. I didn't return his call."

This seemed to surprise Chase. "Why didn't you?"

Lesley swallowed tightly and shrugged. "I couldn't see that it would do either of us any good."

"You were afraid to, weren't you?"

It shocked her that he would know her so well after such a short acquaintance. "Yes," she admitted in a husky murmur. "I was afraid."

"Is that why you contacted me?"

He wanted his pound of flesh, she realized, and at the same moment knew she'd give it to him. "I don't love you, Chase."

"It's a bit difficult to care for another when your heart belongs to a married man."

He made it sound so cold, so cut-and-dried. And ugly.

"He wasn't married when I fell in love with him," she argued, defending herself.

"He is now."

"I don't need you to remind me of that," she cried, raising her voice for the first time.

"Good," he said after a moment, and then repeated himself softer, with less conviction.

"How are the interviews going?" she asked, hoping to make light conversation and gain the information she needed.

"All right." He set the wineglass aside as if he were preparing to leave.

"Would you be willing to look at another application?"

"Probably not." He stood and shoved his hands deep in his pants pockets. "I've got more than I can deal with now. Are you going to recommend a friend of yours?"

"No." Lesley closed her eyes and forced herself to continue. "I was hoping you'd consider marrying me."

Chapter Seven

"You?" Chase repeated slowly, unsure if he was hearing her correctly. It seemed too good to be true, something he dare not believe.

"That's right." Lesley was standing now, her steady gaze nearly level with his own. She studied him as closely as he was studying her. "I'd be willing to marry you."

"Why?" Fool that he was, he had to ask, although he was confident he knew her answer. He wondered if she'd be honest enough to admit it, or if she'd sugarcoat it in order to dupe him.

"I like you very much," she continued, carefully choosing her words. "It's obvious there's some physical phenomenon going on between us. I don't generally respond to a man the way I have you."

He gave her no reassurances nor did he discourage her. She was rubbing her palms together, a nervous habit of hers he'd noticed before. "Those are the only reasons?" he pressed.

"No." She was irritated with him now and he felt relieved. The more emotion she revealed the better. "I don't want to live in Seattle any longer."

She disappointed him. "Isn't marrying a man you don't love a little drastic? If that was your problem, all you need do is apply for a teaching position elsewhere. I'm not up on these things, but I seem to remember hearing that teachers were in high demand all across the country. Try Montana. That's where your mother's living, isn't it?"

"I don't want to move to Montana. I'd rather be in Alaska with you."

"You still haven't answered my question."

"Damn it, Chase Goodman. You're going to make me say it, aren't you? You want to see me crawl and I'm not going to do it. Now do you or do you not want to marry me?"

There'd never been a single doubt in Chase's mind. He knew exactly what he wanted and he had from the beginning. He wanted Lesley. It had always been Lesley and that wasn't going to change.

"It's Tony, isn't it?" he continued, as unemotionally as he could. Funny he'd never met the man and already he despised him for what he'd done to Lesley and for the mind games he continued to play on her. "You're afraid he has the power to reduce you to something you find abhorrent. He wants you, doesn't he? But he's married and that means you'll be his mistress and you're frightened out of your wits that you'll do it because you love him so damn much."

"Yes, damn you, yes." Angry tears glistened in her eyes and her hands were clenched into tight fists at her sides.

"You think marrying me and moving to Alaska is the answer to all your problems."

"Yes," she cried. "I've never lied to you, Chase, not even when it would have been convenient. You know exactly what you're getting with me."

"Yes, I do," he answered softly.

"Well," she pressed with an indignant tilt of her chin, "are you going to marry me or not?"

"Is this a take-it-or-leave-it proposition?"

"Yes."

"All right," he said, walking away from her. "We'll be married Wednesday evening."

"Next week!" She made it sound as if that were ridiculous. Unthinkable. "I couldn't possibly put together a wedding in that amount of time. My mother and Ken are traveling across the south this summer in their trailer. I won't be able to get in touch with them before then."

"Do you want them at the ceremony?"

"Not if it means ruining their vacation plans."

"Then we won't tell them until they're home." If Lesley was looking for arguments and excuses, he'd willingly supply them.

"I'd like to invite a few friends and have a small reception."

"That's fine with me. The hotel can arrange whatever you want with little more than twenty-four hours' notice." Which was about all the time Chase intended on giving her. Any more than that and she might well talk herself out of it. He didn't want to chance that.

"What about the invitations?"

"I'll have a messenger service hand deliver them."

"But they'll need to be printed, and…oh, Chase, there are so many things. I have a dress, but I don't know if you'd want me to wear it since I bought it for another man, but it's so beautiful and—no, I couldn't possibly wear it, and that means I'll need to buy another. It took me weeks to find the first one."

Chase held his breath until his chest ached with the effort. "It seems to me you're looking for excuses."

"I'm not. I swear I'm not. It's just that…"

"Be very sure, Lesley, because once we say those vows there's no turning back. Understand?"

She nodded slowly. "What about all my things? What will I do with them? I couldn't possibly cram everything I own in a couple of suitcases."

"Pack what you want and I'll have everything else shipped. You won't need the furniture, so either sell it or give it away—whichever you want."

"All right."

"We'll need to apply for the wedding license first thing tomorrow morning."

"Okay." She didn't sound overly enthused but he refused to let that bother him. As she claimed, he knew what he was getting and by the same token, she knew what he wanted.

"I'll be by before ten to pick you up," he continued.

She nodded and he started toward the door.

"Chase."

He turned around, impatient now and not understanding it. Lesley had agreed to marry him and that was more than he had expected. "Yes?"

"Would you mind kissing me?" Her voice was small and uncertain. He purposely hadn't made this easy on her for the simple reason that he wanted her to know her own mind. He would have liked to kiss her senseless, and use their mutual attraction to convince her to follow him to the ends of the earth and share his life. It would have been too simple, especially if they were in the throes of several heated kisses, but he couldn't, wouldn't, have allowed that.

What he'd forgotten to take into consideration was that Lesley had taken a giant step toward him; the least he could do was meet her halfway. She needed some reassurances and he should have given them to her long before now.

He walked back to her, framed her face with his hands and claimed her mouth. She opened to him spontaneously, without reserve, and the kiss deepened and deepened until Chase's control teetered precariously.

Damn, but her touch was potent. He'd forgotten exactly how good she felt in his arms. It shouldn't be like this. With every other woman he'd always been composed and in control. His response to Lesley worried him. The fact he found her so damned desirable was important, but that he could easily lose his head over her was a negative.

Lesley exhaled, that soft womanly sigh that drove him to distraction, and he eased his mouth from hers and concentrated on the nape of her neck, scattering kisses there while struggling with his own composure.

"Thank you," she whispered. The beauty of her words and the sweetness of her mouth were fatal to his control.

"This will be a real marriage, Lesley," he warned.

"I realize that." She sounded offended, but Chase wasn't willing to leave room for doubt.

"Good. I'll pick you up first thing in the morning, then."

Lesley nodded and Chase experienced a hollow victory. She'd agreed to marry him, but for none of the reasons he would have liked. She was running away from a painful situation that was destined to bring her heartache.

He was the lesser of two evils.

It wasn't the most solid foundation for a marriage, but with time and patience and love, that mortar would harden.

"You're getting married!" Lori and Jo Ann repeated together in stunned disbelief.

"I didn't offer to buy you lunch in a fancy restaurant for nothing," Lesley commented brightly, digging her fork into a slice of chicken in her hot chicken-and-spinach salad. "What are you two doing Wednesday evening?"

"Ah . . . nothing," Lori murmured.

"Not a thing," Jo Ann agreed.

"Great, I'd like you both to stand up for me at my wedding. Chase and I are—"

"Chase?" Jo Ann broke in abruptly. "Who the hell is Chase?"

"I didn't know you were dating anyone," Lori said, sounding more surprised than upset.

Neither of her friends had touched their seafood Caesar salads. They sat like mannequins, staring at Lesley as if she'd announced she was an escaped convict.

"Chase Goodman," Lesley repeated casually between bites. "That's the name of the man I'm marrying."

Lori, dark and fawnlike, with the most incredible dark eyes, gnawed on her lower lip. "Why does that name sound familiar? Do I know him?"

"I doubt it. Chase's from Alaska."

"Alaska." Jo Ann said the name of the state in a low, uneasy voice, as if trying to remember something important. She reached for her fork. "Did either of you happen to see the news story last week about this guy who came down from Alaska and advertised for a—" She stopped, her eyes widening until they dominated her face. Her throat worked and made odd sounds, but nothing that could be understood as intelligible words.

"You're marrying the guy who advertised for a wife?" Lori looked from Lesley to Jo Ann and then back again, her head moving so quickly that her features blurred.

"Lesley, my dear, have you gone bananas?"

"I suppose." She wasn't going to argue with her two best friends. A week earlier she'd thought the whole idea of marrying a stranger was crazy. She'd said as much to Chase, belittled the women who'd applied, even made derogatory remarks about the type of man who'd dare to defy convention in such an outlandish manner.

One week later, she'd agreed to be his bride.

Lesley didn't have a lot of arguments to offer. "You will be my bridesmaids, won't you?"

"Of course, but—"

"No buts. The wedding's on Wednesday. I don't have time for arguments, and please, don't try to talk me out of this because you can't. My mind's made up. Chase and I are leaving for our honeymoon following the wedding ceremony. From there we're heading to Twin Creeks where Chase lives. He has to be on the job in eight days and that doesn't leave us much time."

"Pinch me," Lori said to Jo Ann, "because this doesn't feel real. We're not actually hearing this, are we? Lesley, this isn't like you."

Now that Lori had spoken her mind, Jo Ann took a turn. "It's because of Tony, isn't it? You're far too sensible to do something like this otherwise."

"I wasn't going to say anything," Lori whispered, rearranging the salt-and-pepper shakers atop the cream-colored linen tablecloth, "but Tony phoned me. He's worried about you, Les. He said he'd been trying to get in touch with you, but you weren't returning his calls."

"Tony's been calling you?" Jo Ann, bless her heart, sounded outraged. "That man makes me wonder. Does April know about this?"

"She's out of town."

"That dirty, stinking rat."

"I knew when he married April that the relationship would never last," Lori said with a faint hint of self-righteousness.

Lesley laughed, grateful for her friends' loyalty. "You suspected it wouldn't last because Tony wasn't marrying me. If he had, you would have both been singing his praises."

"I'm beginning to think Daisy might be right about him," Jo Ann said thoughtfully, stabbing her fork into the crabmeat, and eating with a fervor now. "How was she able to see through him so quickly? The three of us work with the guy nine months out of the year and we have to be hit over the head before it dawns on us that Tony isn't playing fair."

"What did you tell Tony about me?" Lesley casually inquired, although her interest was anything but indifferent.

"Nothing much, just that I'd talked to you recently and you sounded upbeat and happy.

"He seemed surprised to hear that and said he was afraid you were depressed and avoiding people. He sounded genuinely concerned and guilty over the way he'd hurt you. I..."

"Yes," Lesley prompted.

"I felt sorry for him by the time we hung up."

"Sorry for him?" Jo Ann asked, incredulous. "Why would you feel sorry for Tony? He was the one who broke Lesley's heart and married someone else."

Lori shrugged, and looked mildly guilty herself. "He never said as much, but I had the feeling he regrets marrying April. She's never been very friendly toward the three of us and it makes me think she's not a very good wife to Tony."

"Who can blame her for being unfriendly?" Lesley was the first one to defend April.

"Tony made her situation impossible at school," Lori agreed. "We each did our best to make her feel welcome, but we'd all worked with Lesley before and April knew that. She barely attended any of the faculty functions after the wedding. My bet is that she's a really nice person, if she ever gave anyone the chance to know her."

"She gave Tony plenty of chances, don't you think?" Jo Ann muttered, unwilling, even now, to forget the upheaval the arrival of the new first-grade teacher had brought into their lives.

"You haven't talked to Tony yourself?" Lori asked, ignoring Jo Ann's pettiness. For that, Lesley was grateful.

"Not since school's been out." She felt good about resisting the temptation to phone him, but it had required a heavy emotional price. Facing the truth about oneself demanded that. "I won't, either," she added, her resolve growing stronger each minute.

"Good." Jo Ann was in total agreement. Lori looked uncertain.

"Aren't you curious about what he wants?"

"Get real, Lori. What do you think Tony wants?" Jo Ann asked.

Lori studied her for a disbelieving moment. "You don't really think that, do you?"

"Lori, wake up!" Jo Ann said sarcastically and snapped her fingers. "When a married man phones a woman when his wife's out of town, there's only one reason."

"I hesitate to think Tony would do that."

Lesley felt the same way, but she couldn't allow her tenderness for Tony to mislead her. Jo Ann might be skeptical, but her friend's thinking aligned with Daisy's.

"Stop." Jo Ann raised both hands and made a crossing motion with them. "We've veered from the subject at hand and that's Lesley's wedding plans."

"'Lesley's wedding plans,'" Lori echoed, sending a shocked, dismayed look to Jo Ann.

"Are you in love with Chase?"

"No." Lesley refused to be anything but honest with her friends. When it came to her mother and Ken she was willing to elasticize the truth, subtly of course, but she'd never be able to fool her friends. Her mother was another story; she'd trust Lesley was madly in love because that was what she wanted to believe.

Lori's jaw fell open. "You don't even love him."

"I've only known the man a little more than a week. It's a bit difficult to develop a deep, emotional attachment in that amount of time."

"You're willing to marry him anyway," Jo Ann murmured thoughtfully. "That tells me a good deal. He's obviously got something going for him."

"He's good with kids, and gentle." Those were only two of Chase's character traits that appealed to her. Honesty was another.

"What's he look like?" Lori was anxious to know, scooting forward in her chair in her eagerness to learn all she could about the man Lesley would soon be marrying.

"A little like you'd expect someone from Alaska to be. He's tall and muscular and his eyes have a roguish tint to them. He's a comfortable sort of person to be with, entertaining and funny. When he laughs it comes deep from his diaphragm."

"You're marrying a man because he laughs from his belly?"

It sounded absurd, but in part she was. Chase had a wonderful sense of humor and Lesley found the quality important in any relationship, but vital in a marriage.

"You really like this guy, don't you?"

Lesley nodded. It surprised her how much she did care for Chase.

"I was hoping you'd both have time to shop with me this afternoon," Lesley said, pulling herself away from her introspection. She hadn't spoken a word about the type of kisser he was. The man should win awards for his style. She'd never known a man could arouse such a heated reaction with a few tender kisses.

"You're honestly going to go through with this, aren't you?" Even now Lori didn't seem to believe it was true.

"Yes, I am." She looked toward Jo Ann, expecting an argument, unsought advice or words of caution, but her fellow teacher didn't give her one.

"I almost envy you," Jo Ann remarked instead. "This is going to be an incredible adventure. You'll write and let us know what happens, won't you?"

Lesley laughed and was surprised when she felt tears gather in the back of her eyes. Through all the pain and difficulties of the past year, she'd been blessed with truly tremendous friends.

"I wonder what Alaska will be like," Lori said dreamily. "Do you think Twin Creeks will have a friendly moose wandering through town the way they do in the opening of that television show?"

"Hi," Lesley said, letting herself into the house. Chase had spent the afternoon at her rented home, supervising the packers so that her things would be ready for the shippers when the time arrived for her personal items to be transferred north.

He tossed aside the magazine he was reading and smiled up at her. It was the same roguish gleam in his eyes that she'd been telling her friends about only a few hours earlier, and her heart reacted with a surprising surge of warmth.

"How'd your meeting with your friends go?" Chase asked.

"Great." It was ridiculous to be shy with him now.

"They didn't try to talk you out of the wedding?"

Lesley grinned and sat down on the sofa that would soon belong to Daisy and her boys and scooted next to Chase. "I'll admit they were shocked, but once I told them what a fabulous kisser you are, they were green with envy."

"You aren't going to change your mind, are you?"

Lori and Jo Ann had asked her the same question and she gave the same answer now as she had then. "No. Are you worried?"

"Yes." His voice was gruff and he reached for her, kissing her hungrily.

Lesley could find no will to resist him. He'd only kissed her once since she'd agreed to be his wife and she needed his touch, longed for it. She leaned forward and braced her hand against his chest. The hard, even feel of his pulse against her palm reassured her that he enjoyed their kisses as much as she did. At least she wasn't alone in this.

Chase gripped hold of her waist and pulled her closer until her breasts were flattened against his chest. Her nipples hardened immediately.

His kiss was slow, deep and thorough. And not nearly enough.

Chase started to pull away and she protested. "No..."

His mouth came back to hers once more, desperately seeking, hungry for her. She parted her lips to him, inviting the sweet invasion of his tongue, giving him her own. The tip of hers met the tip of his and they danced and curled around one another. By the time Chase pulled away from her, she was weak and dizzy and breathless all at once. Her heart was pounding like the hooves of a stallion slapping across the dry prairie.

"Lesley, listen," he whispered, and pressed his forehead to hers.

"No," she whispered back. "Just hold me a few minutes more. Please." She didn't want to talk, not then, nor was she interested in thinking because if she analyzed too carefully what she was doing, she just might change her mind.

All Lesley wanted or needed was to feel. She longed for Chase to hold her into the next millennium. When she was in his arms she could feel again. For months she'd been trapped, not dead and yet not alive, either, but lost somewhere in between until her emotions were stretched so thin, she felt nothing. No laughter. No tears. Just a numbness that sapped away her energy and destroyed her dreams.

Then she met Chase and suddenly she was laughing again, dreaming again. When he kissed her, a kaleidoscope of feelings flooded her heart. At first she didn't know what was happening to her; she wasn't completely sure how to explain it or if she should even try.

The kisses, which had started slow and melting, quickly gained momentum until the fires they stirred were raging out of control. Chase's tongue was consuming her mouth, his kisses hard and urgent. Lesley wound her arms around his neck and simply hung on, letting the white-hot passion burn away any resistance.

In her need, in her passion-drugged mind, she would have given Chase everything, would have taken from him. What they shared was a basic human need. She yearned for him to fill the aching loneliness of her soul, to reconstruct the tattered threads of her pride.

Chase needed her, too. She would reciprocate generously and without reserve because she wanted him as badly as he wanted her. Only she needed him to hurry and he didn't seem to share the same urgency. She unfastened the buttons of his shirt and when his fingers fumbled with hers, she set aside his hands and opened her blouse herself. She unsnapped her bra and when her breasts fell forward, his hands closed over and cupped them, fondling their weight in his palms.

He stopped kissing her then and buried his face in her neck. His breathing was hard and heavy.

Then, without warning, he broke away from her, leaving her breathless and stunned. Before she could analyze what was happening, he was on his feet and moving toward the door, fastening his shirt as he went. "I have to go."

"Go? But why?"

He paused, his back to her. "Because if I stay I'm going to have you flat on your back on a mattress so damned fast you won't know what's happening."

"I know what's happening."

"Maybe, but I doubt it."

"You . . . you don't want to make love to me?"

Chase didn't answer. He knew why he had resisted the temptation to make love to Lesley. Secretly, he still feared she wouldn't go through with their marriage. If he made love to her—even once—he knew he'd never be able to let her go.

Lesley had sounded like a hurt little girl and couldn't help it. She'd felt safe with Chase, and now he was turning away from her, rejecting her. She'd lowered her guard, offered him everything she had to give and he was walking away from her. The old pain, the old hurt was there with a flesh pain. The six-year-old child whose father had walked away from her was back, chanting her fears. Lesley wanted to place her hands over her ears and tell that grieving little girl to be quiet, but she wouldn't have been heard over the din of her pain.

"Go, then." She buttoned her blouse in world-record time, her fingers working fast and furiously.

He paused at the front door and his shoulders slumped forward. "I can't leave you now."

"Sure you can."

He turned back and walked over to the sofa, sitting down next to her. He pulled her into his arms, disregarding the token fight she put up, and held her. She tried to twist away, but he wouldn't allow it. After a while she gave up the effort. The little girl in her wanted to push him away, hurt him for hurting her. But the womanly part of her needed his comfort.

Chase kissed the crown of her head when she sighed and nestled in his arms.

"You tempt me, Lesley Campbell, more than any woman I've ever known."

"You tempt me, too."

She felt his smile and was glad he was there with her.

"Becky Bright, the newswoman who did the interview with me phoned earlier this afternoon," he told her.

She heard the regret in his voice and wondered at it.

"She wants to do an interview with the two of us right after the wedding. Do you mind?"

"I suppose not. Do you?"

"I mind like hell, but it's the only way I can think to stop the phone calls. According to the answering service, they're still coming in."

"Still?"

"I had the billboard taken down last week and there are more women phoning now than ever. I'm sure some have called before and were discouraged when they didn't hear back right away. Several were phoning to see if I'd made a decision and others wanting to know it if was too late."

"It's certainly been an interesting experiment, hasn't it?"

"Yes, but it isn't one I care to repeat."

Lesley jabbed him with the sharp point of her elbow. "I certainly hope not!"

Chase laughed, tucked his arms around her waist and nuzzled her neck. "I'm going to have my hands full with one wife."

"What about the applicants?"

"I had Sandra write up a form letter and mail it out."

"To eight hundred women."

Lesley felt his smile against her skin. "Not exactly."

"What do you mean?"

"I got eight hundred calls, yes, but not all of them were from women who were looking to be my wife. Through the course of this, I found at least a hundred or more were from mothers looking to introduce me to their daughters.''

Lesley stilled. "I hope you're joking."

"I'm not. There were a few calls from a few disgruntled husbands, as well, who said they'd be willing to give away their wives."

"What a rotten thing to do."

"And more crank calls than I care to mention."

"All right," Lesley said, feeling a bit cocky. "When you come right down to it, just exactly how many serious applications did you receive?"

"One."

"One, but you said . . . I heard on the news."

"Yours was the only one I took seriously."

His words were sweet and soft and exactly what she needed. She rewarded him properly by easing back her head, looping her arms around his neck and directing his mouth to hers. Their kisses were slow and lazy and tasted of warm honey.

Chase wasn't ready to leave for another hour. He needed to finish up some last-minute details with the answering service and the billboard company. Lesley lingered with him on the front porch for ten minutes, neither of them eager to separate even for a few hours.

"I'll be back," he promised. "Where would you like to go to dinner?"

Lesley smiled and kissed the underside of his chin. "Are you in the mood for another hamburger and a rematch at the golf course?"

"You're on, woman."

Lesley remained on the porch until his car was out of sight. She glanced at her watch and realized that within twenty-four hours they'd be married.

The house felt empty without Chase. Funny but she'd lived here for three years, utterly content to be on her own, enjoying her independence. Her whole life felt different now that she was marrying Chase.

She showered and changed clothes, and was packing her suitcase when the doorbell chimed. Her steps were light and eager as she traipsed across the living room. Chase could come in without the pretense of waiting for her to let him in. She should have said as much.

Her smile was bright and her heart full when she opened the door.

"Hello, Lesley."

Her heart, which had seemed light and full seconds before, plummeted like a deadweight to the pit of her stomach.

"Hello, Tony."

Chapter Eight

"Lesley, oh, Lesley." Tony's hands reached for hers, gripping them tightly. "You don't have any idea how good it is to see you again. I've been desperate to talk to you. Why didn't you return my calls?"

The attraction was there, the way it had always been. It shouldn't have surprised her, but it did. Lesley had hoped and fervently prayed that when she saw Tony again, she wouldn't experience this terrible need. With concentrated effort, she jerked her hands free.

"Lesley." Tony's eyes rounded with hurt disbelief.

"I didn't return your calls for a reason. We don't have anything to discuss."

"That's where you're wrong. Lesley, love..."

"I'm not your love."

"But you are," he continued in a hurt little boy manner, as though her words pained him, as though he couldn't believe she would speak to him in this manner. "You'll always be my love . . . you always have been."

"You're married to April." He seemed to need to be reminded of that, and so did she. The strength of her love for him, despite his marital status, was nearly overwhelming. All the things she'd struggled to hide threatened her now.

"I know . . . I know." He sounded uncertain and sad, a combination that never failed to touch a tender part of her heart. Part of her longed to invite him into her home and listen to his troubles, but she dare not and knew it.

"I'm making a new life for myself," she insisted, steeling herself from the pleading she read in his eyes.

"One without me?"

"Yes. Please, Tony, just leave." She eased back, intending to close the door, but he placed his foot over the threshold, blocking her attempt.

"I can't," he insisted. "Not until I've talked to you. Not until you've listened to everything I have to say."

"Tony, please." This was harder, so much harder than what she'd imagined it would be. He must have sensed how difficult because he edged closer.

"Tony." Her voice wobbled with the force of her desperation. "We have nothing to say to one another."

"Lesley."

Chase's voice sounded like an angel's harp. She was so grateful he'd arrived that she nearly burst into tears.

"Chase," she said, breaking away from Tony and rushing forward. She must have appeared desperate, but she didn't care. Chase was her one link to sanity and she held on to him with both hands.

"What's going on here?" Tony demanded. "Who's this man?"

"Actually, I was about to ask you the same thing," Chase said stiffly.

"I'm Tony Holifield."

Lesley felt Chase stiffen at her side as soon as he recognized the name. He reacted by possessively placing his arm around Lesley's shoulders and pulling her closer to his side, stamping her with the seal of ownership. Under different circumstances, Lesley would have enjoyed being linked with Chase this way, but not when he was using it to rub Tony's nose in the fact she belonged to him.

"Who is this man?" Tony demanded.

Lesley opened her mouth to explain, but before she could utter a single syllable, Chase spoke.

"Lesley and I are about to be married."

"Married?" Tony laughed as if he'd just heard a good joke. "You can't be serious."

"We're dead serious," Chase responded.

"Lesley?" Tony looked to her to deny everything.

"It's true," she said with as much conviction as her heart would allow. Unfortunately, it wasn't much.

"That's ridiculous. You've never mentioned anyone named Chase before and I know for a fact you couldn't have been dating him before school was out. Isn't this all rather sudden?"

"Not in the least," Chase said as if they'd been an item for years.

"Lesley?"

"It's amazing the things you don't know about my fiancée," Chase said, smiling down at her.

It was all Lesley could do not to cry out for them both to stop playing these ridiculous games. Tony regarded her with a pained, tormented expression, as if he were the loyal one and she had betrayed him. Chase wasn't any better. The full peacock plumage of his male pride was fanned out in opulent display.

"You couldn't possibly be marrying this man," Tony said, ignoring Chase and concentrating on her instead.

"I already said I was." She hated the way her voice shook. Chase didn't seem overly pleased with the lack of enthusiasm in her trembling response, but that couldn't be helped.

"The ceremony's scheduled for tomorrow," Chase added.

"Lesley, for the love of heaven, you don't care for this man," Tony continued, his gaze burning into hers. Disbelief crowded his eyes.

"You don't know that," Chase challenged.

"I do know it. Lesley loves me. Tell him, sweetheart. You'd be doing us both a grave disservice if you didn't tell him the truth."

Lesley could see no reason to confess the obvious. "I'm marrying Chase."

"But you love me," Tony insisted, his voice agitated and unnaturally high. She noticed that he clenched his fists at his sides as if his temper were on a short rein. He would fight for her if necessary, he seemed to be saying.

"You're already married," Chase reminded Tony with what sounded like a good deal of delight.

Tony concentrated his efforts on Lesley once more, ignoring Chase as if he didn't exist. "Marrying April was a mistake. That's what I've been trying to tell you. If only you'd returned my calls, then you would have known. I love you, Lesley. I have for years. I don't know what came over me.... I can see now that April and I were never right for one another. I've been miserable these last few months without you."

"You don't need to listen to this," Chase hissed in her ear. He tried to steer her past Tony and toward the front door, but she was rooted to the spot and unable to move.

"For heaven's sake, you've got to listen," Tony pleaded, "before you ruin both our lives."

"Where's April now?" Chase demanded.

"She left me."

"You're lying." Chase's voice was tight with barely restrained anger. "You claimed she was visiting her mother for a week."

"She phoned and said she's not coming back. She knows I love Lesley and she can't live with that any longer. It's a blessing to us all."

"If you believe him," Chase said to Lesley, "there's a bridge in Brooklyn you might be interested in buying."

"I'm telling you the truth," Tony insisted. "I should never have married April. It was a tragic mistake on both our parts. April knows how I feel about you. She's always known. I can't hide it anymore, I can't go on pretending. April can't, either. That's why she went to visit her mother and that's why she's decided not to come back."

"I'm marrying Chase." Her voice wavered, but not her certainty. She couldn't trust Tony, couldn't believe him. Chase was right about that. He'd lied to her before, and hadn't dealt fairly with her. The experience had taught her painful but valuable lessons.

"Lesley, don't," Tony cried. "I'm pleading with you. Don't do something you'll regret the rest of our lives. I made a terrible mistake. Don't complicate it with another."

"She doesn't believe you any more than I do."

"The least you could do is have the common decency to give us the privacy to speak," Tony shouted, frustrated and short-tempered.

"Not on your life."

"You're afraid, aren't you?" Tony challenged. "Because Lesley loves me and you know it. You think if you can keep her from listening to me that she'll go through with the wedding, but you're wrong. She doesn't need you anymore, not when she's got me."

"But she hasn't got you. In case you've forgotten, you're married."

As he was talking, Tony stepped closer to Chase, his stance challenging.

Chase dropped his arm from Lesley's shoulder and eased toward Tony. The two men were practically chest to chest. It wouldn't take much for the situation to erupt into a street brawl.

"Stop it, both of you," Lesley demanded. "This is ridiculous."

"You love me," Tony insisted. "You can't marry this barbarian."

"Just watch her," Chase returned with a wide, indolent smile.

"I'm not doing anything until both of you stop behaving like six-year-olds," Lesley insisted. "I can't believe either one of you would resort to this childish behavior."

"I'll divorce April," Tony promised. "I swear by everything I hold dear that I'll get her out of my life."

"I'd think a husband would hold his wife dear," Chase said in a sidebar comment. "Apparently that isn't so. Your vows meant nothing to you the first time. What makes you so sure they will on a second go-around?"

"I'm trying to be as civil as I can about this," Tony insisted, "but if you want to fight this out man-to-man, then fine."

"Anytime," Chase said, grinning broadly as if he welcomed the confrontation, "anyplace."

"Fine."

They were chest to chest once more.

Lesley managed to wedge herself between them and braced a hand against each of their chests. "I think you should go," she said to Tony. It was useless to try to discuss anything now. She wanted to believe him, but Chase was right and she knew it. The first message Tony left claimed that April was away for a week visiting her mother. He hadn't said a word about his marriage being a mistake or that he continued to care for her. But those weren't the kind of things one said into an answering machine.

"I'm not leaving you, not when you're set on making the biggest mistake of your life," Tony insisted. "I already promised I'd divorce April. What more do you want me to do? The marriage was a mistake from the first! What else can I do? Tell me, Lesley, tell me and I'll do whatever it takes to make amends to you."

"I believe the lady asked you to leave," Chase said with the same easy grace. "That's all she wants from you—nothing more. Get out of her life."

"No."

"It'll give me a good deal of pleasure to assist you."

Lesley wasn't sure how Chase managed it, but he grabbed hold of Tony's arm and twisted it behind him. Tony yelped with pain, but had no option but to allow Chase to steer him toward his parked car.

Lesley stood on the porch, her teeth sinking into her lower lip as she watched the unpleasant scene. She was furious and didn't know who to direct her anger toward, Chase or Tony. Both had behaved like children fighting over playground equipment on the school grounds. Neither one of them had shown any maturity in dealing with an awkward situation.

They exchanged a few words at Tony's vehicle and it looked for a moment as if a fistfight was about to erupt, but in the end, Tony climbed inside his car and drove away.

Lesley was pacing her living room when Chase entered the house. "How could you?" she demanded.

"How could I what? Treat lover boy the way he deserved, you mean?"

"You weren't any better than he was. I expected more from you, Chase. The least you could have done was be civil about the whole thing. Instead you acted like a jealous lover." She continued pacing, otherwise she wouldn't have been able to stand it. Her anger created an energy within her that refused to be ignored.

"Did you want to talk to him alone?"

"No."

"Then what did you expect me to do?"

"I don't know," she cried. "Something different than strong-arming him."

"You sound like you wanted to invite him in for tea and then sit around the living room and discuss this like civilized adults."

"Yes," she cried. "That would have been better than a shouting match on my front porch. The two of you behaved as though I were a prize baseball card you both wanted. Tony had traded me away and now he wanted me back and you weren't about to see that happen."

Chase went still, and grew unnaturally quiet. "Is that what you wanted?" he asked.

"No, of course it isn't."

"He can't stand the thought of losing you."

"He was the one who ended the relationship, not me. It's over, Chase. It has been for a long time."

Chase walked over to the window and stared outside. He didn't speak for a long time and seemed to be carefully weighing his thoughts.

"You...you told me once that you had a problem when a woman played one man against another. I'm not doing that, Chase. I wouldn't. You're the man I'm marrying, not Tony."

"You love him," Chase said, turning to face her, "although God knows he doesn't deserve your devotion. You could have lied to me about your feelings, but you haven't and I'm grateful."

"I don't trust Tony," she whispered, "but I do you."

"You might not trust him, but you *want* to believe him, don't you?"

"I...I don't know. It doesn't matter if I do, does it? I've already agreed to be your wife and I'm not backing out of this marriage." She refused to do to Chase what Tony had done to her. She wasn't willing to push him aside in favor of Tony's promises. Chase was right. Tony had always been a sore loser, no matter what the stakes.

Chase said nothing for several moments. "The choice is yours, and I'll abide by whatever you want. I want you, Lesley. Don't misunderstand me. It surprises me how very much I desire you. If you agree to marry me, I promise you I'll do my damnedest to be a good husband to you."

"You make it sound like I haven't made up my mind. I've already told you—and Tony—that I'm going through with the wedding."

"It isn't too late to call it off."

"Why would I want to do that?" she asked, forcing a laugh that sounded as if it had cost her the earth to make light of this. In many ways it had.

"Because you're in love with Tony," Chase answered with sober, dark eyes focused on her. "Think this through very carefully," he advised and walked to her door.

"You're leaving?" She feared Tony would return and she didn't know what she would do if Chase wasn't there to buffer his affect on her heart, if Chase wasn't there to help her.

"Will you call me in the morning?" he asked. He didn't need to explain what it was he expected to hear from her. That was obvious. If she was willing to go through with the ceremony then she should let him know.

"I can tell you that right now," she said, folding her hands together in an effort to keep from reaching for him.

"You might feel differently later."

"I won't. I promise you I won't." The desperate quality of her voice was all the answer he seemed to need.

He walked over to her, placed his hands on her shoulders and brought her into his arms. "I shouldn't touch you, but I can't make myself walk out that door without kissing you. Forgive me for that, Lesley." His last words were whispered as he lowered his mouth to hers. His lips settled over hers with a gentle kind of desperation. Her mouth parted under his and the kiss was filled with a longing and a hunger that left her breathless and yearning for more.

"Goodbye, Lesley." He expelled his breath forcefully, turned and walked away.

Lesley watched him go and had the feeling she might never see him again. The pain that struck her with the thought felt like a sucker punch.

Her knees were trembling and she sank onto the sofa and buried her face in her hands.

He'd lost her, Chase realized as he unlocked the door to his hotel suite. He could have taken the advantage and run with it. At first he thought he would do exactly that. Tony wasn't right for Lesley—anyone could see it.

All right, he reasoned, he believed it so strongly because he wanted her for his own. Maybe the weasel *was* good for Lesley, although Chase couldn't see it himself.

To Chase's way of thinking, Tony would string her along for years. He'd promise to divorce April but there'd be complications. There were always complications in these matters, and Lesley's heart would be stripped naked by the time Tony was free. If he ever managed to follow through on his promises. Chase knew exactly whose best interests Tony had, and those were his own.

Tony might hold some genuine affection for Lesley, but he didn't really love her. He couldn't possibly, otherwise he'd never put her through this agony.

Then again, Chase's own intentions weren't exactly saturated in holy water. He needed a wife and he wanted Lesley. It didn't matter to him that she was in love with another man; all that mattered was her willingness to marry him and live with him in Alaska.

If there was a law against selfishness, he'd be swinging by his neck, right next to that bastard Tony.

So he'd done the only thing he could and still live with himself in the weeks to come. Damn, but this being honorable had proven to be hard. It was much more difficult than he'd anticipated.

He'd given Lesley both the freedom and the privacy to make whatever choice she wanted. He wouldn't stand in her way, judge or condemn her if she opted not to go through with their marriage.

He was about to lose the wife he wanted and nobility was damn little compensation.

All he needed to do was wait until she'd made up her mind. He had the distinct feeling this was going to be a very long night.

"It shouldn't be this hard," Lesley wailed to her no-nonsense neighbor.

"You're right. It shouldn't," Daisy agreed. She stood next to Lesley's refrigerator and braced one hand against her hip. "Look at it this way. You could let Chase go back to Alaska alone and spend the next year or two being lied to, manipulated and emotionally abused by a bona fide rat. Or," she added with a lazy smile, "you could marry a terrific man who adores you."

"Chase doesn't adore me."

"Maybe not, but he's crazy about you."

"I'm not even sure that's true."

"Have you got eyes in your head, woman?" Daisy asked sarcastically. "He chose you out of hundreds of women."

"Not exactly...."

"Listen, if you want to argue with someone, let me bring in the boys. They love it and are much better at it than either of us. I don't have time to play silly games with you. I'm calling this the way I see it. If you want to mess up your life, that's your choice."

"I don't," Lesley insisted.

"Then why are you having such a hard time phoning Chase? You said he was waiting to hear from you."

"I know, but . . ."

"Is there always going to be a but with you?" Daisy demanded impatiently. "Now call the man before I get really mad."

Smiling, Lesley reached for the phone. She prayed she was doing the right thing. After wrestling all night with the decision, she woke and tearfully called Daisy, sobbing out her sorry tale. Daisy, who was already late for her classes, had listened intently. Her neighbor seemed to know exactly what Lesley should do. She made it all sound so crystal clear and easy. It should have been, but it wasn't, even now with the telephone receiver pressed to her ear.

"Hello."

"Chase, it's Lesley. I'm sorry to phone so early, but I thought you'd want to know as soon as possible."

There was a slight hesitation before he spoke. "It would simplify matters."

"I . . . want to go through with the marriage this evening."

"You're sure?"

He had to ask. Why couldn't he have just left matters alone? Instead he seemed to want to complicate everything. "Yes, I'm sure." Her voice shook as if she were on the verge of tears.

Daisy took the receiver from her hand. "She knows what she's doing, Chase. Now don't you worry, I'll have her to the church on time." Whatever Chase said caused Daisy to laugh. After a couple of moments, she replaced the receiver. "You going to make it through the day without changing your mind?"

"I . . . don't have any choice, do I?"

"None. If you decide to stand that man up at the altar, I'm going to murder you and marry him myself. The boys would be thrilled and we both know it."

Lesley laughed. "All right. I'll see you back here at four. Don't be late, Daisy, I'm going to need all the support I can get."

"What if Tony calls you?"

"He probably will, but fortunately I don't plan on being here. I've got a million things to do before five and I don't intend to waste a single moment on Tony Holifield."

"Good." Daisy beamed her a bright smile, and was out the door moments later.

Being nervous came as a surprise to Chase. He fully expected to stand before the preacher he'd hired and say his vows without a qualm. When it came to making Lesley his bride, he didn't suffer doubts or regrets, just nerves.

When she first arrived with her close friends for the simple wedding ceremony, Chase hadn't been able to take his eyes off her. He'd never seen a more beautiful woman. He'd rented a tuxedo although what had prompted the action was beyond his comprehension. The tie felt like a tight ring around a small-mouth canning jar and the cummerbund reminded him of a girdle. He knew Lesley would be pleased though, and when she smiled at him, he was glad he'd made the effort.

She'd chosen a soft peach dress, overlaid in white lace. She didn't wear a veil but a pretty pearl headpiece with white silk flowers that curled over the side of her head. The bouquet of baby roses was clenched in her hands.

It was all rather informal. With time restriction being what it was, they didn't have a choice. Lesley introduced

Chase to her friends and he shook hands with each one. Then within a matter of minutes it was time for the ceremony.

They stood with everyone gathered around them in the middle of the room. The minister said a few words of introduction about the sacrament of marriage, its significance, and then asked them in turn to repeat their vows.

It was at that moment that Chase fully comprehended what was transpiring between Lesley and himself. He pledged before God that he would love Lesley, meet her needs, both physical and emotional. In essence he'd vowed to help her be everything that God intended.

The responsibility boggled his mind. He'd given Lesley time to weigh the decision before agreeing to be his bride, never dreaming he needed to ponder the deed, as well.

He looked to Lesley as she said her vows. Her steady gaze met his and her voice was strong and clear, without hesitation. When it came time, he slipped the gold band on her finger. He noticed tears brightened her eyes, but her smile reassured him. He could only hope these were tears of joy and not regret.

When he received permission to kiss his bride, Chase gently took her into his arms and kissed her. With everyone watching them, he made sure it was a short, powerful kiss. He also made sure it carried a punch, his tongue invading her lips and sweeping her mouth.

Lesley's eyes were laughing when they broke apart. "You'll pay for that later, Chase Goodman," she promised in a fervent whisper.

Chase could hardly wait.

There was enough food to feed fifty people. He wasn't sure how many would come and so he'd had the hotel staff handle everything. Lesley had given him the names of her friends and there were several people he'd invited, as well, including Sandra and her husband.

Becky Bright was there, along with her cameraman. Lesley was wonderful during the interview, answering the questions without so much as a hint of nervousness. He suspected it was her training as a teacher that made her so comfortable with strangers. Personally he was grateful she dealt with the reporter because he was at a loss for words.

The ceremony itself was a formality in his mind, something that was necessary and nothing more. He compared this wedding with waiting in a long line for a ticket to a good play: the best part had yet to come.

Now he wasn't so sure.

The vows had gotten to him. He hadn't taken the seriousness of his commitment to Lesley to heart until he realized that these promises were more, much more, than a few mumbled words. They were vows, a contract made between Lesley and himself.

"I've never seen a more beautiful bride," he told her while they were going through the buffet line. It seemed they hadn't had a moment alone all evening. His heart was crammed full with all the things he wanted to say to her, and couldn't.

"I've never seen a more handsome groom," she whispered back and when she looked at him, her eyes softened.

Chase dished up his plate. "I meant what I said." He knew that sounded melodramatic and a little trite, but he couldn't keep it to himself any longer.

"About what?" Lesley added a cherry tomato to her plate.

"The vows. I wasn't just echoing a bunch of meaningless phrases, I meant them, Lesley. I'm going to do everything within my power to be the right kind of husband to you.''

She didn't look at him, didn't move, and he wondered, briefly, if he'd frightened her with his seriousness, or perhaps shocked her. "Lesley?"

"I'm sorry," she whispered brokenly, staring down at the bowl of pasta salad as though it were filled with diamond chips.

"I shouldn't have told you that." She was suffering from pangs of guilt, he reasoned. The ceremony obviously hadn't affected her the way it had him.

"No... Oh, Chase, that was the most beautiful thing you could have said." She raised her gaze to his and he realized she was struggling to hold back her tears. "I meant it too, every word. I'm eager to show you how good a wife I intend to be."

Until the moment Lesley had walked into the hotel, Chase wasn't entirely certain she would show for the wedding. All day he'd attempted to brace himself in case she did change her mind. Now she was his wife, and there was no turning back for either of them.

"Where are you going for your honeymoon?" Daisy asked, filling her plate from the opposite side of the buffet table.

"Victoria," Chase answered. He hadn't said anything to Lesley, wanting to surprise her. That didn't seem important now.

"Victoria," she repeated. "Oh, Chase, what a wonderful idea."

"I don't imagine you're going to do much sight-seeing though," Daisy added with a suggestive chuckle.

"Daisy!" Lesley said, blushing becomingly.

Their honeymoon. The words floated through his mind like a balloon. Not knowing if Lesley would ever show for the wedding, he'd put off all thoughts to what would follow afterward.

He'd wanted to make love with Lesley almost from the first moment they'd met. But he was determined not to wander into the physical side of their relationship until they were both ready to deal emotionally with that aspect of their lives together. He didn't know about Lesley, but he was more than ready. More than eager. He only hoped she was, too.

Their guests didn't seem the least bit anxious to leave. The champagne flowed freely, but Chase drank only a small amount. He needed a clear head.

They left, under a spray of rice and birdseed. He placed Lesley's suitcase in the back of his rental car and raced around to the front of the vehicle.

"Ready?" he asked, smiling over to his wife. His wife. Even now the word felt awkward in his mind. Awkward, but very right. He accomplished what he'd set out to do. He'd gotten himself a bride.

Chapter Nine

"The honeymoon suite," Lesley whispered as the bellhop carried in their suitcases. "You booked us the honeymoon suite?"

Chase gave the bellman a generous tip and let him out the door. "Why are you so surprised? We're on our honeymoon, aren't we?"

"I know, but, oh, I don't know." She walked around the room and ran her hand over the plush bedspread on the king-size bed. "Oh, Chase, look," she said after she walked into the bathroom. "The tub's huge."

"Imagine wasting all that water," he teased, enjoying her excitement.

"They left champagne and chocolates, too."

"I'll file a complaint. How are any two people supposed to survive on that? A man needs real food."

"There's always room service."

"Right," he teased, "I forgot about that."

"Oh, Chase, this is such a lovely surprise." She seemed shy about touching him, stopping just short of his arms. He was a bit embarrassed himself, although he hadn't stopped to analyze why. Lesley was his wife and he was her husband.

"I... I think I'll unpack," she said, reaching for her suitcase.

"Good idea." There was definitely something wrong with him. Lesley should be in his arms by now, panting and begging him to make love to her. Instead, they were standing back to back emptying their suitcases as though they had every intention of wearing all those clothes.

"Are you hungry?" he asked, just to make conversation.

"No, but if you want to order something, go ahead."

"I'm fine." The hell he was. His temperature was rising by the minute all for want of her.

"I think I'll take a bath," she suggested next.

"Great." He realized after he spoke that she might find his enthusiasm vaguely insulting, but by the time he thought to say something she was in the bathroom.

The rushing sound of running water filled the suite. He noted she left the door ajar, but he wasn't completely certain she'd done so on purpose.

Focusing his attention on unpacking, Chase opened and closed several drawers, but his mind wasn't on putting his clothes in any order. His thoughts were with Lesley in the other room.

Lesley removing her clothes.

Lesley stepping naked into the big tub.

Lesley sighing that soft, womanly sigh of hers as she slipped her luscious, ripe body into the steaming water.

The powerful image was so strong that Chase sagged onto the edge of the mattress. He didn't know what the hell was the matter with him. They were married and he was acting like a choirboy, afraid of his own shadow.

"You need me to wash your back?" he asked.

"Please."

Chase's spirits lifted. That sounded downright encouraging. He smoothed back his hair, stuck his hand in front of his mouth and tested his breath before advancing into the other room.

Lesley was exactly as he'd pictured her. She was resting her back against the tub, surrounded by a floating layer of frothy bubbles.

The scent of blooming roses wafted up at him like mist off the moors. Her pink toes were perched against the far end. The welcome he read in her eyes made his heart beat so fast and furiously that for a moment he couldn't breathe.

"How's the water?" he asked, stuffing his hands in his pants pockets.

"It's wonderful."

"I suppose you've added a bunch of woman's stuff in that water."

"Woman's stuff?"

"Bath oil, perfume—that sort of thing."

"Do you mind?"

"Not in the least." It was driving him slowly insane, but that didn't trouble him nearly as much as the peekaboo view he had of her soft, pink body. She raised one knee from the water and the bubbles slid down her oil-coated leg in a slow, tantalizing pattern.

Her knee was bright pink and warm and for the life of him, he couldn't stop staring at it. For the life of him he couldn't stop thinking about that same knee wrapped around his waist while he was buried so deep inside her that...

"The water looks inviting." His tongue nearly stuck to the roof of his mouth he was so damned excited.

"Would you care to join me?"

His heart was doing that crazy pounding again, sort of a drumbeat gone crazy. "You wouldn't mind? I mean..." Hell if he knew what he meant. "Should I bring the champagne and chocolates?"

"Just the champagne. Let's save the chocolates for later."

He nearly stumbled out of the room in his eagerness to give her what she wanted. He opened the bottle and the popping sound echoed like a small explosion. His hands trembled as he poured them each a tall flute of champagne. He carried them into the other room. He handed her the glass and sipped from his own, badly needing the courage it offered. It took him a moment to realize Lesley hadn't tasted hers.

"I'll wait until you're in the bath with me," she explained.

"Oh." Not until then did he realize he would need to undress. He did his damnedest not to be self-conscious about it, but didn't know how well he succeeded. He wasn't normally shy, but he'd lived alone for a good many years and generally when he undressed there wasn't someone watching his every move.

His shorts proved to be the most embarrassing. His erection was as hard as steel and had been from the moment he heard Lesley running the bathwater. He didn't try to hide his desire, coyness was beyond him, but he was grateful she didn't call attention to it, either.

He stepped into the tub and she scooted forward to make room for him. He eased himself into the hot water, positioning himself behind her. She was slippery in his embrace and he tucked his arms around her torso and brought her up against him until her back was tightly pressed to his chest. He brushed his mouth over her hair and relaxed, closing his eyes.

"You feel good," he whispered, which had to be the understatement of the century. Surely heaven had to be something close to this.

Lesley nestled against him and as she did, the underside of her breasts brushed against his forearm. He lifted his arm slightly and was rewarded by having two pink delectable nipples peep just above the waterline. He lowered his forearm and the same perky nipples disappeared again. That wasn't to his liking, he decided, and raised them again, only higher this time so that the full lushness of both breasts was exposed.

Lesley had gone still and so had he. It was as though they'd both lost the need to breathe. He cupped her bare breasts and she sighed as if this was what she'd been waiting for, as if she wondered what had taken him so long.

Damned if he knew.

He smiled, not from amusement, but with male pride and satisfaction. Lesley wanted him, too, but felt just as inept at letting him know. They were certainly a pair.

"You feel like silk," he whispered, rubbing his hand down her smooth abdomen until it disappeared beneath the bubbles. Her legs stirred restlessly and she turned her head toward him, inviting his kiss.

Chase didn't disappoint her. He bent forward and kissed her slowly, seducing her mouth with his own. Soon he didn't know who was seducing whom. They were both breathless by the time he lifted his head.

Chase felt as though a fire was burning through him and had settled in his loins. His erection was so hard that it thrust against her. Using his arms for leverage, Chase brought Lesley farther up his chest until she was practically on top of him. She lifted her hips to assist him and her buttocks settled over the heated length of his staff. Chase groaned inwardly, every movement of her buttocks against him was the purest form of torture he'd ever experienced. She must have realized it because she moved often and with deadly accuracy.

He slid his hand from her abdomen to the juncture between her legs. Her thighs parted eagerly at his touch. Dear sweet heaven, she was hot and moist, hotter than the water. He concentrated on luring her with her own pleasure, gently rubbing her most sensitive spot. She sagged against him and from the soft whimpers she repeatedly made, he knew he'd succeeded beyond his expectations.

When his finger entered her, she whimpered and lifted her hips almost out of the water, twisting around and seeking his mouth with her own. They kissed, the urgency of their need centered on their mouths as she buckled beneath him, gasping and moaning.

Chase broke off the kiss; his arousal by this time had reached a point so painful that he gritted his teeth. In one swift motion he stood, taking her with him. Water sloshed over the sides of the tub, but Chase could have cared less. He carried Lesley to the bed and placed her on the mattress, not caring if they were soaking wet or that they left a watery trail from here to kingdom come.

He framed her face between his hands, his gaze locked with hers as he positioned himself over her and slowly, relentlessly buried himself as deep inside her as he could go.

The pleasure was so keen, it was almost more than he could bear, almost more than he could resist. He nearly exploded right then.

Lesley's inner muscles clenched at him, massaging his heat, and that strained his self-control all the more. He arched his head back in a desperate effort to regain some semblance of control.

She was hot and slick, inside and out. And tight. Sweet heaven she was tight. The effort it cost him not to climax was beyond measure. Sweat broke out against his brow as they moved together simultaneously. Her body answered each of his thrusts by raising her hips from the bed until Chase felt his sanity slowly, surely eroding away.

His hoarse moans of pleasure mingled with her soft whimpering cries and he was lost. He panted as he convulsed against her, damning himself for not lasting longer.

He waited a moment to catch his breath before framing her face with his hands once more. He kissed her again and again, his passion deep and urgent as if his need for her was as great as it had been only moments earlier. And it was.

Already he could feel himself growing hard again. It surprised Lesley as much as it did him.

"Chase?" she whispered.

"I'll go slow and easy this time," he promised, tucking his hands beneath her buttocks and lifting her against his erection. He withdrew and reentered her in increments, one hot inch at a time. His pleasure was immense, but nothing could have given him more gratification than watching Lesley.

She was panting, her head arched back, her breasts exposed to him like a tribute, an offering he couldn't refuse. Her nipples were hard and seemed to be throbbing, begging for his attention. He bathed each one with his tongue and was rewarded with a soft sob of pleasure.

When he was buried in her to the very hilt, until he felt the mouth of her womb, he slid his hands under her buttocks and worked her against his thrusts. Slow and easy, he repeated over and over in his mind, wanting to return a hundredfold the pleasure she had given him. But in the end, it proved to be useless. He'd trusted that he'd last much longer this time, that the dire urgency of his need had been met the first time, but he was wrong.

His release came like a cataclysmic explosion out of nowhere. His blood ran so hot and fast that it felt as if it would sear his veins.

Lesley whimpered and repeatedly kissed his face, mumbling the same words over and over again, but he couldn't understand what she was saying. Not that it mattered. Her words echoed what was in his own heart.

When it was over, he rested his forehead against hers, his breath harsh and uneven. He could find no words to explain what had happened. No woman had ever satisfied him so completely. No woman had ever brought him to the point of no return the way Lesley had.

Whatever was between them, be it commitment or love or something he couldn't define, it was completely outside of his control.

Everything with Lesley was beyond his realm of experience. Everything with her was going to be brand-new.

Buchart Gardens was breathtakingly beautiful. Chase and Lesley spent their first morning as man and wife walking hand in hand along the meandering paths, over the footbridges and through the secret corners of the gardens. Lesley couldn't ever remember seeing any grounds more beautiful, with a profusion of so many varieties of flowers that she soon lost count.

By the time they broke for lunch, Lesley was famished. Chase was too, gauging by the amount of food he ordered.

"I've got to build back my strength," he told her.

Lesley didn't know she was capable of blushing, not after the wondrous night they'd spent. She didn't know it was humanly possible for any two people to make love so fervently or so frequently. Just when she was convinced she'd never survive another outburst of pleasure, he'd convince her in the most profound way that she could. And she did.

"You're blushing." Chase sounded shocked.

"Thank you for calling attention to it," she chided. "If one of us is blushing, it should be you."

"Me?"

She leaned across the table, not wanting anyone to overhear. "After last night," she whispered heatedly.

"What about last night?" His voice boomed like a cannon shot, or so it seemed to Lesley.

"You know," she said, sorry now for ever having introduced the subject.

"No, I don't, you'd better tell me."

"You ... a superman."

He grinned and wiggled his eyebrows suggestively.

"Chase," she admonished.

"As soon as we've finished lunch, let's go back to the hotel."

"But we've only seen half of the gardens," she protested, but not too strenuously.

"We'll come back tomorrow, I promise."

"It's the middle of the afternoon."

"So?"

"It's ... early." The excuse was token at best. She couldn't fool him, nor could she fool herself. She wanted him as badly as he wanted her. It was crazy, insane. Wonderful. A woman dreams all her life of finding a man like this.

"Don't look at me like that," Chase said with a soft groan.

She gave herself a mental shake. "Like what?"

"Like you can't stand to wait a minute longer."

She lowered her eyes, embarrassed and frustrated. "I don't think I can."

He swore under his breath, stood abruptly and slapped some bills down on the table. "Come on," he said, "let's get out of here."

"We came on the tour bus, remember?"

"We'll get a taxi back."

"Chase—" she laughed "—that'll cost a fortune."

"I don't care what it costs. If we don't leave now we could well be arrested. There are laws against people doing in public what I intend to do to you."

Lesley was sure her face turned five shades of red as they hurried out of Buchart Gardens. They located a taxi and the second after Chase gave the driver the name of their hotel, he brought her into his arms. His kiss was wet and wild, and thorough. Thorough enough to hold them until they got back to the hotel.

Chase paid the driver and they raced hand in hand into the hotel and through the lobby, not stopping until they reached their room.

Chase's hand shook when he inserted the key and Lesley's heart was touched by his eagerness.

"This is the most insane thing I've ever done in my life," she said, trying not to laugh. It was crazy, but it was also wonderful.

The door swung open and Chase brought her inside, closing the door and backing her against it.

"I was going to go berserk if I couldn't touch you the way I wanted," he whispered, kissing her with a hunger that nearly bruised her lips.

"We both must be crazy."

He reached behind her and found the small button at the nape of her neck, his rough hands struggling awkwardly to unfasten it. Reading the desire in his eyes, she pushed his hands aside, undid the button and brought the blouse over her head. Carelessly tossing it aside, she unsnapped her bra, freeing her plump breasts for his exploration.

He groaned and Lesley swore she never heard a more erotic, passionate sound. She closed her eyes as his hands cupped her breasts. His mouth followed. He captured her nipple between his lips, tonguing it, teasing it, sucking at it until she was convinced she would faint.

"Chase…" She wasn't sure what she wanted, only *that* she wanted.

Apparently he knew, because he scooped her into his arms and carried her to the bed as if she weighed no more than a puppy. He removed her slacks and his own. He made a low, almost guttural sound as he slid between her legs and filled her.

Lesley arched her hips upward and cried out when he entered her. Slowly, panting because she found it impossible to breathe and experience such keen pleasure both at once, she lowered her buttocks back to the mattress.

Chase seemed to need this time to come to grips with the sensation, as well. As soon as he had, his hips began to move in a pagan rhythm. Tucking her legs around his waist, Lesley sighed as he thrust deeper and deeper inside her.

This was what she wanted, what she craved. Chase inside of her, sliding deeper and deeper. Chase hot and heavy, her body trapped beneath his. This was what she was crazy for. At least they shared this craziness. She wasn't alone in this.

Alone.

Lesley smiled to herself and buried her face in her husband's neck, using her tongue in the most provocative way. With Chase she would never be alone again. With Chase she was whole, complete. It happened then, a wild eruption of pleasure that shattered whatever composure she had managed to maintain. She buckled beneath him and sobbed with her release.

Seconds later he climaxed and sagged against her. They didn't speak; they didn't need to. After a moment, he tried to roll from her, but she tightened her arms and legs around him and wouldn't let him leave her.

"I'm too heavy for you," he protested.

She needed the feel of him, needed the reality of this man, this moment. She pressed her hands to his face and with tears she couldn't explain blurring her vision, she looked up at him.

"Thank you," she whispered.

He kissed her, his touch gentle and caring.

"What's happening to us?" she asked, thinking he could help her understand.

"What do you mean?"

"Is this just good sex or is it more?"

"More," was his immediate response.

"Do I love you?" It wasn't the question he expected her to ask, which was fine since it surprised even her.

"I don't know."

"Are you in love with me?"

His brow creased as if the question required fervent consideration. "I know I've never felt this intensely for any woman. What's happening between us, this physical thing, is as much of a surprise to me as it is you." He leaned forward and kissed the tip of her nose.

"I'm pleased you decided to marry me," Chase continued, "although if this continues much longer, I may be dead within a year."

Lesley laughed and, wrapping her arms around his neck, lifted her head from the mattress just enough to kiss him. The kiss was long and sweet.

"You're pure magic," he whispered against her lips.

"Me?"

He grinned.

She answered him with a grin of her own. "I don't know about you, but I'm starving."

Chase nuzzled her nose with his. "Let's not take any chances this time and order room service. It's ridiculous to continue to pay for meals I never have a chance to eat."

After a long, leisurely lunch, they played tourist for the rest of the day, but didn't wander far from the hotel. They'd learned their lesson, it seemed. They had high tea at the Empress Hotel, toured the wax museum, explored the undersea gardens.

They crammed as much as they could into the afternoon and returned, exhausted, to their hotel early that evening.

"Where do you want to go for dinner?" Chase asked.

"Dinner?" Lesley demanded. "I'm still full from tea."

"I'm a growing boy, remember?"

"You couldn't possibly be hungry."

He slipped his hand inside her blouse and flicked his thumb over her nipple. "You'd be surprised."

She tossed aside her head and glared up at him. "You're joking, right?"

"What do you want to do?"

There wasn't a doubt in her mind. "Soak in a long, hot bath and take a nap. You kept me up half the night, remember?"

"A bath?" His eyes rounded, eagerly.

Despite her exhaustion, Lesley smiled. "Later," she promised and kissed him sweetly. "Give me an hour or two to regroup, okay?"

His face fell in mock disappointment.

"Come on," she said, holding her hand out to him. "You can nap with me, if you promise to go to sleep." She yawned loudly and pulled back the covers. The bath would come later. Right now it would only bring temptation for them both.

"I dreamed we'd be in bed by five o'clock," Chase muttered, "but I never thought it would be to sleep. Some honeymoon this is turning out to be."

"Some honeymoon," Lesley agreed, pressing her head against the thick feather pillow and closing her eyes. Within seconds she could feel herself drift off.

The phone beside the bed rang, startling Lesley so much that she nearly toppled off the mattress. Before she could assimilate what was happening, Chase reached for the receiver.

"Hello," he answered gruffly. Whoever it was calling caused him to laugh. He placed his hand over the mouthpiece. "It's Daisy."

"Daisy?" Lesley said into the receiver, surprised to hear from her neighbor.

"Trust me, I wouldn't be calling if it wasn't necessary."

"Don't worry. You weren't interrupting anything."

"Wanna bet?" Chase said loud enough to be sure to be heard at the other end of the line.

"Listen, Lesley, this isn't my idea of a fun phone call, but I figured you'd better know. Tony's been pestering me for information about you and Chase."

Lesley sat up in the bed. "You didn't tell him anything, did you?"

"No, but the movers arrived while he was here and I saw him talking to the driver. He might have been able to get information out of him."

"I doubt it," she said, gnawing on her lower lip. "Those men are professionals. They know better than to leak out information about their clients."

"Having that segment about you and Chase on television this evening didn't help matters any. Tony phoned two seconds after the piece aired."

Lesley groaned. She'd forgotten about that.

"What's wrong?" Chase wanted to know.

Lesley placed her hand over the mouthpiece. "Nothing."

"Daisy didn't call for no reason," he argued.

"I'll explain later," she insisted, although it wasn't a task she relished.

"It's Tony, isn't it?"

"Chase, please."

"All right, all right," he grumbled, but he wasn't happy and didn't bother to disguise the fact. He climbed out of the bed and reached for his clothes, dressing with an urgency she didn't understand.

"Okay, I'm back," she told Daisy.

"Tony's looking to make trouble."

"He said as much earlier. I shouldn't be surprised."

"I don't know why I'm so worried," Daisy muttered. "It isn't like he could do anything. You're already married."

"You wouldn't have called if you believed that. What do you think he's going to do?"

She felt Daisy's hesitation. "I don't know, but I felt I should warn you."

"Thanks," Lesley said, genuinely grateful. Tony seemed a million light-years away. In space and time and with her emotions. Only a couple of days earlier she was convinced she loved him. That wasn't true any longer. She did harbor feelings for him, but it wasn't love.

"So?" Daisy said, her voice dipping suggestively. "How's the honeymoon?"

Lesley closed her eyes and sagged against the velvet headboard. "Wonderful."

"Are you two having fun with one another?"

"Daisy!"

"I meant sight-seeing and all."

"I know exactly what you meant," Lesley chastised.

"If that's the case, why are you trying to be coy?"

"All right, if you must know, we're having a very good time. There—are you satisfied?"

"Hardly. I've got to tell you, Lesley, I could be jealous. It's been so long since I made love, I feel like a virgin all over again."

Lesley laughed. "If Tony gives you any more trouble, let me know and I'll get a restraining order."

"You'd do that?" Daisy sounded absolutely delighted.

"In a heartbeat."

Chase stood on the other side of the room, his back to her. Lesley watched him for a moment and said to her neighbor, "Listen, we'll talk as soon as we get back."

"Which is when?"

"The day after tomorrow, but we'll be flying up to Alaska almost immediately. Keep in touch, okay?"

"I will," Daisy promised and ended the conversation a few moments later.

Lesley replaced the receiver. Her hand lingered on the phone while she mentally composed what she was going to say to Chase.

"So it was Tony," he commented, turning back to her.

"Yes. He's making a pest of himself." Chase's hands were in his pockets and he looked unsure. Of her and their marriage. It seemed a bit early to be having doubts, and she said as much.

"The bastard wants you."

"I know, but I married you." Her words didn't seem to reassure him any.

Kneeling on top of the mattress, Lesley pressed her hands against her stomach. "I'm starved. How about you?"

Deep in thought, it took Chase several moments to respond. When he did, he shook his head.

"I suggest those chocolates and a hot bath," Lesley murmured.

That got his attention, and his gaze locked with hers and she burst out laughing. "Come here," she said, holding her arms out to Chase. "It's time you understood that neither one of us has anything to fear from Tony. I've made my decision and chose to be your wife. A jealous ex-fiancé doesn't stand a chance."

Chase stood where he was, as if he wasn't sure he should believe her, as if he wasn't sure this was possible.

Lesley had no qualms about going to him. She rose out of the bed and was halfway across the room before she realized she was nearly nude. It didn't bother her—she was proud of her body. Chase had made her feel that way. Her attention was focused on the man in front of her, not on herself.

Stepping up on her toes, she kissed him lightly, her mouth feathering his.

"Lesley..."

"Shhh."

He stood perfectly still, and with his eyes closed, he allowed her to continue rubbing her mouth over him. When she was satisfied with his lips, she kissed the underside of his jaw, dragging her mouth down his neck, then up to his ear. After what seemed like an eternity, he threaded his fingers through her hair and raised her face to his.

"I want you to be very sure."

"I am," she promised. "I am sure."

After a couple of moments he raised his head and his gaze found hers. "A hot bath and chocolate sounds like an excellent suggestion."

Lesley smiled contentedly. This marriage business was turning out far better than she'd ever imagined.

"Where are we going?" Lesley insisted. They'd left Victoria that afternoon and had traveled down the Kitsap Peninsula and taken the ferry across from Bremerton to Seattle. Lesley had assumed they'd be heading directly back to her house. If that was the case, then Chase was taking an interesting route.

"There's something I want you to see."

She glanced at her watch, and swallowed her impatience. They'd gotten a later start than what they'd anticipated. Their morning had started out with a hot bath. At least the water had started out hot, but by the time they finished it had cooled considerably. Because their schedule was off, they'd been forced to wait for a later ferry.

Their airline tickets to Alaska were scheduled for first thing the following morning and Lesley had a hundred small details she needed to take care of before then.

"There," Chase said, pulling into an asphalt parking lot and parking.

"Where?" She hated to be obtuse, but she didn't see anything.

"The billboard," he said.

Looking up, she noticed the original billboard Chase had used to advertise for a wife. The sign had been changed and now read, in huge black letters, THANK YOU, LESLEY, FOR SHARING MY LIFE.

"Well?" he asked, waiting for her to respond.

"I . . . Oh, Chase, that's so sweet and so romantic. I could cry." She was struggling to hold back the tears.

"I want to make you happy, Lesley, for the rest of our lives." He brought her into his arms and kissed her.

Happiness frightened her. Every time she was truly at peace, something would happen. Life would demand some toll, some pain. It had started when she was a child. She'd never been happier than the week before they were scheduled to leave for Disneyland. Not only had the trip been canceled, but she'd also lost her father.

She'd been genuinely excited about her wedding to Tony, planning the details, shopping for her wedding dress and choosing her clothes. Then he'd broken the engagement.

Lesley was happy now, and she couldn't help wonder what terrible price it would cost her this time.

Chapter Ten

Lesley's hand reached for Chase's as the airplane circled Fairbanks, Alaska, before descending to the airport. Lesley had found the view of Alaska's Mount McKinley, in Denali, awe inspiring. After living in Seattle, between the Cascade and the Olympic mountain ranges, to have Denali impress her was saying something. The tallest peak in North America rose like a jewel from the land far below, crowned by a halo of clouds. Her peak shone bright, kissed by the sun until the snow glittered like diamond dust. Denali stood proud and serene before her lesser subjects much the way Mount Rainier reigns over the Pacific Northwest.

"Is it all so beautiful?" she asked as the plane made its final approach.

"There's beauty in every part of Alaska," Chase assured her, "but some of it's more difficult to see than others."

"I'm going to love Twin Creeks," she said, knowing it would be impossible not to, if the area was anything like the beauty she viewed from the plane above Fairbanks.

Chase's fingers tightened around hers. "I hope you do."

They landed and were met by a tall, burly man with a beard so thick it nearly obliterated his face. Beneath his wool cap, she caught a glimpse of twinkling blue eyes.

"Pete Stone," Chase said casually, placing his arm around Lesley's shoulders, "this is Lesley."

"You done it? You actually done it?" Pete asked, briefly removing his wool cap and scratching his head. His hair was shoulder-length, Lesley noted, and as thick as his beard. "You got yourself a wife?"

"How do you do?" Lesley said formally, holding out her hand. "I'm Lesley Goodman." Pete ignored her proffered hand and reached for her instead, hauling her against him and hugging her so tight, he lifted her three feet off the ground. Lesley wasn't offended as much as she was surprised. She cast a pleading glance to her husband, who didn't look any more pleased with this unexpected turn of events than Lesley did herself.

"Pete," Chase said stiffly. "Let her go. Lesley's not accustomed to being manhandled."

"You're jealous?" Pete said, slowly releasing Lesley. His grin would have been impossible to see beneath the mask of his beard, but his eyes fairly sparkled with delight. "That tells me you care about this little slip of a girl."

Being nearly six feet tall, Lesley had yet to think of herself as a little slip of anything. She couldn't help liking Pete despite his bear-hugging enthusiasm.

"Of course I care for her. I married her, didn't I?"

"You sure did, but then you said you was coming back with a wife if you had to marry yourself up with a polecat."

"Lesley's no polecat."

"I got eyes in my head," Pete argued. "I can see that for myself."

"Good. Now, is the plane ready or not?" Chase asked, reaching for two of their suitcases. He didn't look toward Lesley and she sensed that Chase regretted Pete's mentioning his determination to find a wife. She hadn't accepted his proposal under any misconceptions. If she'd turned him down, he would have found someone else. She'd known that from the first.

Pete picked up the two additional pieces of luggage, and winked at Lesley. "The plane's been ready since yesterday. I flew down a day early and raised some hell. I've been as horny as a lumberjack right before the spring thaw."

"Pete," Chase barked, motioning his head toward Lesley, "don't talk that way in front of a lady."

What she could see of Pete's face reddened immediately. "I meant no offense."

"None taken," Lesley assured him, doing her best to hide a smile. When she could, she fully intended on reminding Chase that in the past few days he'd behaved like a lumberjack, as well.

"Do you mind leaving right away?" Chase asked her as they approached the four-passenger plane.

"No," she assured him with a smile. She was anxious to reach her new home, and she knew Chase was eager to get back. It would have been nice to spend some time in Fairbanks, but they'd have plenty of opportunity for that later.

"So," Pete said to Chase, after they'd boarded the plane, "are you going to tell me how you did it?" The two men occupied the front seats while Lesley stretched out in the back.

"Did what?"

"Got someone as beautiful as Lesley to marry you."

Chase was preoccupied with a series of gadgets. He flipped a number of switches. "I asked her."

Lesley was mildly insulted that he condensed the story of their courtship into a single, unflattering phrase.

"That was all it took?" Pete seemed utterly amazed. He twisted around and looked to Lesley. "You got any single friends?"

"Daisy," she answered automatically, already missing her neighbor.

"Daisy," Pete repeated as if the sound of her name conjured up the image of a Greek goddess. "I bet she's beautiful."

"She's divorced with two boys," Chase supplied absently, "and recently started dating the guy she works with, so don't get your mind set on her."

Pete was quiet for a couple of minutes; silence was a rare commodity with this man, Lesley suspected. "I'm surprised you didn't get yourself a woman with a couple of kids, liking the little rascals the way you do."

"Lesley suits me just fine," Chase said, then reached for the small hand mike and spoke with the air-traffic controller, listing several details and then awaiting his instructions. Within minutes they were in the air.

"Won't it be dark by the time we arrive?" Lesley asked.

Pete laughed as if she'd told a good joke.

"The sun's out this time of year until midnight," Chase explained.

Pete twisted around, tucking his arm against Chase's seat. "Did Chase tell you much about Twin Creeks?"

"A little." Damn little she realized with a start. All she knew was that Twin Creeks was near the pipeline and that Chase was employed by one of the major oil companies. The town was small, but then there weren't any exceptionally large cities in Alaska. The population of Fairbanks, according to some information she read on the plane, was less than eighty thousand.

"You tell her about the mosquitoes?" Pete asked Chase next, his voice low and conspiratorial.

"Mosquitoes?" Lesley repeated. She'd considered them to be a tropical pest. There were plenty around the Seattle area, but then the air was moist and vegetation abundant. She'd never much thought of mosquitoes near the Arctic.

"Mosquitoes are the Alaska state bird," Pete teased, smiling broadly. "You ain't never seen 'em as big as we get 'em. But don't worry, they only stick around in June and July. Otherwise they leave us be."

"I have plenty of repellant at the cabin," Chase assured her, frowning.

"Twin Creeks is near the Gates of the Arctic wilderness park. Chase told you that much, didn't he?"

Lesley couldn't remember if he had or not.

"We're nestled at the base of the Brooks range which is part of the Endicott mountains."

"How long does it take to drive to Fairbanks?" she asked.

"I don't know," Pete admitted, rubbing his beard as he considered her question. "I've always flown myself. We don't have a road that's open year-round, so not many folks drive that way. Mostly we fly. The way people own cars, the folks in Twin Creeks mainly rely on planes for their transportation needs. It's easier that way."

"I see." Lesley was beginning to do just that. Twin Creeks wasn't a thriving community the way she'd assumed. It was a station town with little more than a handful of people. All right, she could live with that. She could adjust her thinking.

"Twin Creeks is on the edge of the Arctic wilderness," Chase explained absently.

It was difficult to read his tone, but Lesley heard something she hadn't before. A hesitation, a reluctance, as if he feared once she learned the truth, she'd regret ever having married him. She suffered no remorse for marrying Chase. It wasn't possible, not anymore. Their honeymoon had seen to that.

"What about the wildlife?" she asked, curious now.

"We got everything you can imagine," Pete answered enthusiastically. "There's caribou, Dall sheep, bears, wolves..."

"Bears?" She refused to listen beyond that.

"They're a damned nuisance if you ask me," Pete continued. "That's why most of us have caches so..."

"A cache?" Lesley interrupted.

"A cache," Pete repeated as if he was sure she must know.

"It's like a small log cabin built on stilts," Chase explained. "It's spelled *c-a-c-h-e,* but pronounced cash."

"Bears and the like can't climb ladders," Pete added. "But they do climb poles, so we wrap tin around the beams to keep them off."

"What do you store there that the bears find so attractive?"

"It's a primitive freezer for meat in the winter."

"I keep extra fuel and bedding in mine," Pete explained. "And anything else I don't want the wildlife getting. You've got to be careful about what you set outside your door, but Chase will explain that to you, so don't worry. We haven't lost anyone to bears in two, three years now." He laughed, and Lesley didn't know if he was teasing or not.

Lesley swallowed uncomfortably and pushed the thought out of her mind. "I think moose are interesting creatures," she said conversationally, remembering Lori's comment.

"We get them every now and again, but not often." Once more it was Pete who answered.

By the time they landed, several hours later, Lesley was both exhausted and worried. After they'd parked the plane in a hangar, and unloaded their luggage, Pete drove them to a cabin nestled in a valley of alder, willow and birch trees. Lesley didn't see any other cabins along the way, but then she wasn't expecting Chase to live on an oak-lined street. Neighbors would have been welcome, but he didn't seem to have any within walking distance.

"See you in the morning," Pete said after delivering two suitcases to the porch. He left immediately, after slapping Chase across the back and making a comment Lesley couldn't hear. She didn't need to be a rocket scientist to figure out Pete was issuing some unsought marital advice.

"You're meeting Pete in the morning?" Lesley asked. Chase had explained that he needed to be back to work. But she hadn't expected him to fly halfway around the world, sleep three hours and then arrive for work as fresh as dew on a morning rose almost immediately after their arrival.

"I have to check in," Chase assured her. "I won't stay away long, I promise." They were standing on the porch and Lesley was anxious to get a first look at her new home. It was difficult to know what to expect from the outside. She'd seen vacation homes that were much larger than this.

Chase unlocked the door and turned to Lesley, sweeping her off her feet as if she weighed no more than the suitcase. His actions took her by surprise and she gasped with pleasure when she realized he was following tradition and carrying her over the threshold.

Lesley closed her eyes and soaked in the splendor of being in his arms. They kissed briefly and Chase carried her into the bedroom and the two of them sat on the edge of the mattress together.

"This has been the longest day of my life," Lesley said with a yawn. "I could kill for a hot bath and room service, but I don't think I'd stay awake long enough for either."

"I've dreamed of having you in this bed with me."

Lesley cupped his face and tenderly kissed his lips. "Come on. I'll help you bring in the luggage."

"Nonsense," Chase countered immediately. "It's no problem. I'll get it."

Lesley didn't object. While Chase dealt with their suitcases, she could explore their home. The bedroom was cozy and masculine looking. The walls were made of a light wood, pine, she guessed, with a double closet with two drawers below each door.

A picture was the only object on top of the dresser and Lesley knew in an instant the couple staring back at her from the brass frame were Chase's parents. The bed was large, too big for the room, but that couldn't be helped.

The floor was wood, too, but there were several thick, braided throw rugs positioned about.

Moving into the living room, Lesley noticed a huge rock-and-cement fireplace. It took up nearly all of one wall. He had a television, which eased Lesley's mind. So there was electricity; she hadn't been sure of that, but had hoped there would be.

The furniture was homey and inviting. A recliner and an overstuffed sofa, plus a rocking chair. Chase loved books, if the overflowing bookcases were any indication.

A microwave caught her eye from the kitchen countertop, which was faded red linoleum, and she moved in that direction. The huge refrigerator and freezer stood side by side and looked new, dominating a large portion of one wall. Most everything else, including the dishwasher and stove, were ancient looking. She'd make the best of it, Lesley decided, but she was putting her word in early. The kitchen was often the very heart of the home and she intended on making theirs as modern and comfortable as possible. From the looks of it, she had her work cut out for her.

"Well?" Chase asked from behind her. "What do you think?"

"I think," she said, turning and hugging her arms around his middle, "that I could get accustomed to living here with you."

Chase sighed as if she'd just removed a giant weight from his shoulders. "Good. I realized as soon as I saw Pete that I hadn't prepared you for Twin Creeks. It's not a thriving metropolis, you know."

"So I gathered. Are there neighbors?"

"Some," he answered cryptically. He held her close, and she wasn't able to read his expression.

"Close?"

"Not exactly. Are you ready for that bath?" he asked, changing the subject, but not smoothly enough for her not to notice.

"Oh, yes." She planned to soak out more hours than she cared to count of being cooped up inside an airplane.

"There's only one problem," he said, sounding regretful. "I don't have a tub."

Lesley stiffened. "I beg your pardon."

"There's only a shower. It's all I've ever needed. At some point we can think about installing a bathtub, if you want."

"No problem." A shower instead of a bath was a minor inconvenience. She'd adjust, given time.

Chase needed to make a couple of calls and while he was busy, Lesley showered and readied for bed. Her husband of four days undressed, showered and climbed into bed with her.

The sheets were cold and instinctively Lesley nestled close to Chase. He brought her into the warm alcove of his arms and gently kissed her hair.

"Good night," Lesley whispered when he turned off the light.

"'Night." The light was off, but it remained bright inside the room. She'd adjust to sunlight in the middle of the night, too, Lesley reasoned. But it seemed that she was going to have to make more adjustments than she realized.

She rolled onto her side and positioned the pillow to cradle her head. Currently she was too tired to care, too tired to do anything but sleep.

Chase, however, had other ideas. Chase cuddled her, his arm slipped over her warm middle and captured a plump breast.

Lesley smiled softly to herself as she felt his manhood swell and harden against her backside. She moved her bottom against him and he muffled a groan. With his free hand, he reached past the elastic of her bottoms, flattening his palm against her tummy, seeming to await her wishes.

Lesley sighed and parted her thighs for him. With infinite care, he lowered his finger toward his quest. Already she was hot and moist and eager for him. She whimpered softly when he reached his objective, readying her.

"You know what I want," he whispered hoarsely close to her ear.

"Yes." She surrendered, rolling onto her back and lifting her arms to him in abject welcome. Indeed she did know what he wanted. By that time she was desperate for him, as well.

Chase woke with the alarm. His eyes burned and he felt as if he were fighting his way out of a fog before he realized what he needed to do to end the noise.

Lesley didn't so much as stir. He was pleased the irritating buzzer hadn't woken her. He'd like nothing better than to stay in bed and wake his wife and linger for several minutes with her at his side.

That wasn't possible though. Not this morning. There'd be plenty of other mornings when they could tarry. He looked with pleasure toward that time.

Chase slipped out of bed and reached for his jeans and shirt. Wandering into the bathroom, he splashed cold water onto his face in a desperate effort to wake. He'd report in to work, do what needed to be done and leave again. It shouldn't take more than thirty minutes, an hour at the most. There was a chance he'd be home even before Lesley woke, which was what he'd like, since he could think of several erotic ways in which to rouse her.

He smiled the whole time he heated himself a cup of coffee in the microwave. He sat in the recliner and laced up his boots, reached for a light jacket and was out the door.

Pete was just pulling around the bend when Chase walked down the two front steps. He sipped from his coffee and walked toward his friend.

"Trouble," Pete greeted.

"What's going on?"

"The hell if I know."

"It isn't going to take long is it?" Chase knew the answer to that already. Nothing was ever easy around the pump station.

"I gotta tell you," Pete said to him good-naturedly, "your arrival back couldn't have been more timely."

Chase released a four-letter word beneath his breath. He'd wait an hour or so, call Lesley and explain. This certainly wasn't the way he wanted their lives together in Twin Creeks to start, but it couldn't be helped. It seemed a shame she would learn the truth so soon.

Lesley stirred awake to blazing sunshine. Funny, that was how she'd gone to sleep, too. She rolled her head toward Chase, surprised to find the other half of the bed empty. Swallowing her disappointment, she tossed aside the bedding and sat on the edge of the mattress.

Chase had parked their suitcases just inside the bedroom. Lesley decided to unpack first thing, and by the time she'd be through doing so, she hoped Chase would be back.

She dressed, then examined the contents of the cupboard for something to eat. As soon as Chase returned, they'd need to do some grocery shopping. With him having been gone for several weeks, they needed to restock the essentials.

The phone rang while she was munching on a dry bowl of cereal.

"Hello," she answered enthusiastically, knowing it likely to be Chase, and she was right.

"Lesley, I've run into some problems here at the station." He sounded as though he was a thousand miles away, his voice tinny and distant.

"Will you be long?"

"I don't know. Do you think you can manage without me for a while?"

"Of course."

"I can send Pete if you'd rather not be alone."

"I'll be fine, and I certainly don't need any babysitter."

He hesitated. "Don't go wandering off by yourself, all right?"

"With bears and wolves roaming about, I'm not likely to take any strolls." It would take an earthquake to get her out the front door, but she didn't tell him that.

Once more she sensed his regret. "I'm sorry about this."

"Don't worry. I'll be fine."

"You're sure?"

"Chase, stop worrying, I'm a big girl."

"I've got to go."

"I know. Just answer one thing. We need groceries. Would you mind if I took your car and drove into town and picked up a few items?'' She eyed her bowl of cereal. ''We need milk, eggs and the like.''

She heard him curse under his breath. ''Groceries. Damn, I didn't think of that. Hold off, would you, for just a bit. I'll be back as soon as I can.''

''Don't worry about me,'' Lesley insisted. She didn't want him fretting about her when she was perfectly capable of taking care of herself. Besides, he had other matters on his mind just then.

''I'll be back as soon as I can.''

''I know.'' She was lonesome for him already, but determined to be a helpmate and not a nuisance.

Another hour passed and she'd completely reorganized their bedroom. She consolidated Chase's dresser to make room for her things and hung what she could in his cramped closet. When Chase had a few minutes to spare, she needed him go through and weed out what he didn't need.

The sound of an approaching car was as welcome as a soft drink in August. She hurried onto the front porch to find Pete approaching the house in his four-wheel-drive vehicle.

''Howdy,'' he called, and waved as he climbed out of the truck. ''Chase sent me to check up on you.''

''I'm fine.''

''He had me stop off and pick up a few things while I was on the way.'' He reached inside the car and lifted two bags of groceries out and carried them toward the house.

''I could have gone myself.'' She was disappointed that Chase didn't trust her enough to find her way around. Just how lost could she get?

''Chase was looking forward to introducing you around town himself,'' Pete explained, walking past her and into the kitchen. He seemed to have read her thoughts. He set the bags down on the counter and Lesley investigated the contents. For being a bachelor, Pete had done a good job of shopping.

"What do I owe you?" she asked.

"Nothing," Chase's friend responded, helping himself to a cup of coffee. "Chase took care of it. He's got an account at the store and they bill him monthly."

"How quaint."

Pete reached for the sugar bowl and added two teaspoons, stirring vigorously. "Chase mentioned you're one hell of a cook."

"Fair to middling," she supplied. Since he didn't show any signs of leaving, she poured herself a cup and joined him at the kitchen table.

"There's plenty of deer meat in the freezer."

"Deer?"

"You never cooked deer before? What about caribou?"

"Neither one." Didn't anyone dine on good old-fashioned beef in Alaska?

"Don't worry. It cooks up like beef and doesn't taste all that different. You'll do fine."

Lesley appreciated his confidence even if she didn't share it.

"So," Pete said relaxing against the back of the chair, his hands encircling the mug, "what do you think of the cabin?"

Lesley wasn't sure how to answer. It was livable, but it wasn't anything like what she'd expected. As she'd said to herself countless times before, she'd adjust. "It's home," she said, trying to be diplomatic about it.

"Chase bought it 'specially for you."

Lesley lowered her gaze, knowing that couldn't possibly be true. He hadn't known her long enough to have chosen this cabin on her account.

"He's only been living here a few months. He decided about March that he wasn't going through another winter without a wife and set about getting ready for one. The first thing he did was buy this place and move off the station."

"Do you live at the station?"

"Nope. I bought myself a cabin, as well, year or so ago.

"Chase has lots of plans to remodel, but he wanted to wait until he found the right woman so they could plan the changes together."

Lesley looked around, the ideas already beginning to form. If they knocked out the wall and joined the living room with the kitchen, they could take away the cramped feeling.

"Chase did all right for himself," Pete said, sounding proud of his friend. "I got to tell you, I laughed when he first told me he was going to Seattle and bringing himself back a wife."

"Why didn't he marry someone from around here?" Lesley asked. It was a question that had plagued her from the first.

"First off, there aren't any marriageable women in Twin Creeks. He might have met a woman in Fairbanks had he tried, but he didn't want to spend his vacation so close to home. Seattle appealed to him far more."

"I'm glad he did come to Seattle."

"He seems downright pleased about it himself. This is the first time I've seen Chase smile in a year or more, ever since his father died. He took it hard, you know."

Lesley pretended she did, although she'd told him about her own parents, she couldn't remember Chase mentioning his.

"So soon after his mother—that's what took him by surprise. He's all alone now and he needed someone to belong to the way we all do. I don't know that he's ever voiced that, but it's the reason he was so intent on marrying."

"What about you?" Lesley asked. "Why haven't you married?"

"I did once, about ten years back, but it didn't work out." Pain flickered in and out of his eyes. "Pamela didn't last the winter. I hope for Chase's sake you're different. He's already sweet on you, and if you left him, it'd probably break his heart."

"I'm not leaving." It would take a lot more than a harsh winter to change her mind about her commitment to Chase. She'd never taken duty lightly and she'd pledged before her friends and God to stand by Chase as his wife, his love, his partner.

"Good." Pete's twinkling blue eyes were back.

"Chase sent you out to baby-sit me, didn't he?"

Pete laughed. "Not exactly. He was a little afraid you were going to get curious and do some exploring."

"Not after the conversation we had about the bears."

"They aren't going to hurt you. You leave them alone and they'll leave you be, too. You might want to ask Chase to take you to the dump and that way you'll get to see them firsthand."

"They hang around the dump?"

"They sure do, sorting through the garbage looking for goodies. We've tried a variety of ways to keep them away, but nothing seems to work and we finally gave up the effort."

"I see." Lesley wasn't impressed. "Has anyone thought to bury the garbage?" The solution seemed simple to her.

"Obviously you've never tried to dig tundra. It's like cement an inch below the surface."

"What's wrong at the station?" Lesley asked, looking at her watch. It was already well past noon.

"I can't rightly say, but whatever it is will have to be fixed before Chase can come home. Trust me, he isn't any happier about this than you. Chase isn't normally a swearing man, but he was cursing up a blue streak this morning. He'll give you a call the minute he can."

"I'd like to see the town," Lesley said. She was eager to meet the other women and become a part of the community. It was too late in the year to apply for a full-time teaching position, but she could make the arrangements to get her certificate and sign up as a substitute.

"Chase will take you around himself," Pete explained. "It wouldn't be right for me to be introducing you."

"I know. Tell me about Twin Creeks, would you?"

"Ah . . . there's not much to tell."

"What about stores?"

He shrugged. "We order most everything through the catalog."

"Obviously there's a grocery store."

"Oh, sure, but it's small."

She wasn't exactly expecting one with a deli and valet parking.

"What's the population of Twin Creeks?"

Pete wasn't one that easily disguised his feelings and it was apparent from the way his eyes darted away from hers that he wasn't keen on answering. "We've had something of a population boom since the last census."

"What was the official total?"

"You might want to talk to Chase about that."

"I'm asking you," she pressed, growing impatient. "A thousand?"

"A little less," he said, drinking down what remained of his coffee.

"How much less?"

"A few hundred."

"All right, five hundred then?"

"Not that many."

Lesley pinched her lips together. "Just tell me and be done with it. I hate these guessing games."

"Forty," Pete mumbled into the empty mug.

"Adults?" Her heart felt as if it'd stopped dead.

"No, that's counting everyone, including Mrs. Davis's cat."

Chapter Eleven

"How many women live in Twin Creeks?" Lesley demanded.

"Including you?" Pete asked, looking decidedly uncomfortable by this time. He set the coffee mug down on the table and sat staring into it as though he expected tea leaves to appear so he could decipher his response.

"Of course I mean including me."

"That makes a grand total of five then." He continued to hold on to his mug as if it were the Holy Grail.

"You mean to tell me there're only five women in the entire town?"

"Five women within five hundred miles, I suspect, when you get right down to it." If his face got much closer to the mug, his nose would disappear inside the silly thing.

"Tell me about the other women," Lesley insisted. She was pacing by this time, her palms rubbing each other so hard and fast that her hands soon started to burn. Chase had purposely withheld the information about Twin Creeks from her. Fool that she was, she hadn't thought to ask, assuming when he mentioned the town that there was one!

"There's Thelma Davis," Pete said enthusiastically. "She's married to Milton and they're both in their fifties. Thelma runs the grocery store and she loves to gossip. You'll get along with her just fine. Gladys Thorton might be something of a problem, though. She's a little crabby and not the sociable sort, so most folks just leave her be."

"Is there anyone close to my age?"

"Heather's twelve," Pete replied fervently, looking up for the first time. "She lives with Thelma Davis. I never did understand the connections. Heather isn't her granddaughter, but they're related in some way."

The woman closest to her in age was a twelve-year-old girl! Lesley's heart plummeted hard enough to crash through tundra.

"You'll like Margaret, though. She's a real social butterfly. The minute she hears Chase brought himself back a wife, she'll be by to introduce herself."

"How old is Margaret?"

"Damned if I know. In her fifties, I'd guess. She doesn't like to discuss her age and tries to pretend she's younger."

"I see."

"I'd best be heading back," Pete said, obviously eager to leave. "I know it's a lot to ask, but would you mind not mentioning to Chase that I was the one who told you? We've been friends for a long while and I'd hate for him to take my spilling the beans to you personally."

"I'm not making any promises."

Pete left as if he couldn't get away fast enough.

An hour later, Lesley still hadn't decided what she was going to do, if anything. Chase had misled her, true enough, but she wasn't convinced that it mattered. She probably would have married him anyway.

No wonder he'd been so interested in Seattle's history and the story of the Mercer brides. Although more than a hundred years had passed since that time, she was doing basically the same thing as those women, moving to a frontier wilderness and marrying a man she barely knew.

Chase arrived shortly after one, looking discouraged and miserable. Lesley met him at the front door and waited, wondering what and how much to say.

Without a word of greeting, Chase pulled her into his arms and his mouth came down on hers. The familiar taste of him was like a small slice of heaven and she opened to him without restraint, without reserve.

"Damn but I missed you," he whispered into her hair, his arms wrapped around her middle.

"I missed you, too."

"Pete brought the groceries? Did he get enough of everything?"

Lesley nodded. "Plenty." She broke away from his arms. "I didn't know your parents were both dead," she said, as a means of easing into their conversation. She slipped her arm around his waist and led him into the kitchen. It went without saying that he was hungry and she opened a can of chili and began heating that for him. It helped to keep her hands occupied so he wouldn't guess she was agitated.

Chase stood with his back against the counter. "My mom passed away a couple of years ago. She died of a heart attack. It was sudden and so much of a shock that my father followed less than a year later. They say people don't die of broken hearts, but I swear that isn't true. My dad was lost without Mom, and willed himself to die.''

"I'm sorry, Chase, I didn't know."

"I meant to tell you."

"It was after her death that you decided to marry?"

"Yes," he admitted, watching her closely. "Does that trouble you?"

"No." Her reasons for accepting his proposal hadn't been exactly flawless. She'd been escaping her love for Tony, running because she feared she was too weak to withstand her attraction to her former fiancé. Recently those reasons had blurred in her mind, fogged in with her doubts and the unexpected happiness she'd found with Chase. They'd bonded on a physical and spiritual level much sooner than she'd anticipated. They belonged together and if it was Tony's craziness that had brought them to this point, that didn't matter. What did was her life with Chase.

"How's everything at the station?" she asked, placing the steaming bowl of chili on the table and taking out a box of soda crackers.

"Not good. We're going to need a part." He wiped a hand down his face and ignored the lunch she'd prepared for him. "I hate doing this to you so soon, but it looks like I'm going to have to go after the motor myself."

"You're leaving?" She felt as though she'd been punched by the unexpectedness of it. "How long will you be gone?"

"I don't know yet. A day, possibly two."

It wasn't the end of the world, but she felt isolated and alone as it was. Without Chase she might as well be floating off on an iceberg.

"When do you have to leave?" she asked, in a whisper.

"Soon. Listen, sweetheart, I don't want this any more than you do, but it can't be helped."

Sweetheart. He'd never used affectionate terms with her before. He was genuinely worried, as well he should be. He was going to have to introduce her to the good people of Twin Creeks sooner or later, and she was confident he'd opt to explain rather than have her discover the truth on her own while he was away.

"I'll pack an overnight bag for you," she offered, half waiting for him to stop her right then and explain.

"Lesley."

She smiled softly to herself, relieved at the hesitation she heard in his voice. He was going to tell her.

He moved behind her, wrapped his arms around her waist and slipped his hand inside her light sweater to cup her breast. He brushed his fingertips back and forth over her erect nipple in a lazy caress. "We won't be able to sleep together tonight."

"Yes, I know." Her voice sounded thick and achy even to her own ears.

He caught her earlobe between his teeth and sucked gently. "One night can be a very long time," he suggested in a heated whisper.

"It won't be so bad."

"It could be, though."

"Oh." Brilliant conversation was beyond her when he touched her this way. Already she could feel her resolve weakening. It frightened her that she was so vulnerable to his will.

His lips nibbled at her ear and hot sensation spread liquid fire though her treacherous body. "I was thinking you might want to give me something to send me off."

"Like what?"

He rubbed his erection against her. "You can use your imagination, can't you?"

Despite her irritation, the red blood of arousal pounded through her veins. She was weak with desire and furious with them both. With Chase, because he was so casual about letting her learn the truth, and with herself, because he could so quickly awaken her senses. She'd never thought of herself as oversexed, but lately she had her doubts.

Lesley closed her eyes in an effort to gather her wits. She could either take the pleasure he was offering or she could confront him and they could deal with the more pressing problems than his libido.

"I was in a foul mood all morning," Chase continued in a whisper, "hurrying because I wanted to get home. It was a new experience wanting to rush home."

"What was the big hurry?"

"Do you honestly need me to say?" He gave a throaty chuckle. "It's never been like this with any other woman. I can't get enough of you. We make love and instead of glorying in the satisfaction you give me, I immediately start wondering when I can have you again. Have you put a spell on me?"

"No." If anything she was the one enchanted.

He turned her to face him, and with trembling hands, lifted her sweater and freed her breasts. His fingertips continued to caress her nipples until they were tight and throbbing. She wouldn't be able to bear much more.

She might have been able to put an end to it if he hadn't chosen to kiss her just then. His kiss was deep and hungry and so completely exhaustive that any shiver of protest instantly melted and dribbled away. She felt boneless and incredibly languid.

He lifted her unresisting body into his arms, and carried her into their bedroom, gently placing her on the mattress. Unsnapping her jeans, he released her zipper and after she'd raised her hips to aid him, he removed her bottoms.

He groaned and swore impatiently under his breath as he unfastened his pants. "Pete will be here in five minutes."

"Hurry, then," she pleaded, "please hurry." The violence of her desire for him was a shock. She savored the richness that she could make him want her so desperately, but the blade was double-edged. She was reckless for him, too.

Chase mounted her and filled her in one swift motion. She lifted her hips to accommodate the power of his thrusts and they sighed in unison, drowning in sensation. Soon they were gasping together in mutual release and satisfaction.

Chase kissed her again and again. It wasn't until he lifted his head and frowned that she knew something was wrong.

"You're crying," he said, gently brushing the hair from her brow and wiping the tears from her cheek with his thumbs.

She looked up at him though the veil of moisture. Closing her eyes, she rolled her head to one side. "Go, or you'll be late."

"I'm not leaving until you tell me what's wrong."

"Pete's coming." She pushed him away and went about the task of redressing.

"He'll wait. Damn it, Lesley, tell me what's wrong." He righted his clothes as well and reached for an overnight bag, stuffing it with the essentials he would need as he waited for her response.

"You tell me what's wrong."

Chase frowned. "You're angry because I have to leave you so soon after we arrived, but, sweetheart, that can't be helped."

She was so infuriated by this time that she knotted her fists at her sides. "Pete told me his wife didn't last out the winter. My sympathy was with Pete and the emotionally weak woman he married. I was making all sorts of judgmental statements in my head, automatically blaming her. That's what's so sad. I blamed her, without the benefit of the doubt. I considered her weak and—"

"What has Pete's marriage got to do with us?" Chase gripped her by her arms and was staring at her intensely. A horn honked just outside and he cast an irritated look over his shoulder.

"Go," she said, freeing herself from his possessive hold. "Just go."

"I can't, Lesley, not with you like this."

She smeared the moisture down her face. "It might have helped if you'd let me know Twin Creeks is nothing more than a hole in the road. There are only five women here. Three of those five are years older than me, the fourth is a twelve-year-old girl and the other one is . . . me."

The car horn was longer and more urgent this time.

"Go on," she said, squaring her shoulders. "Pete's waiting."

Chase wavered, took one step toward the door and then returned to her. "Will you be here when I get back?"

She had to think about that for a moment, then nodded.

He briefly closed his eyes. "Thank you for that." He left then without kissing her. Without touching her. And without saying goodbye.

Lesley ended up throwing the chili she'd prepared for Chase into the garbage. She'd never been fond of it herself although Chase certainly seemed to be if his cupboard was any indication. There was one entire shelf with nothing but cans of chili.

She moved from one room to the next, sniffling and feeling sorry for herself. She'd let the opportunity to talk matters out with him slip through her fingers and all for a quick tumble.

Her cheeks burned with the memory. She'd assumed following their honeymoon that the intensity of their physical longing for each other would diminish to more circumspect levels. It embarrassed her that their means of communication was so base.

Their relationship hadn't started out that way. This was a new development. One that had taken them both by storm.

It had happened that very afternoon. Her desire for Chase had clouded her thinking. Because she'd opted to make love instead of talking matters out, she continued to carry the burden of his deception.

Lesley gloried in those first few days with how frequently Chase wanted her. Her joy was made complete in the ready response he evoked in her. He worked hard to woo her with light touches and gentle caresses, plotting her seduction, but in the process of meeting his demands, she'd fallen into the trap of needing him, too. She desired him so badly that she willingly surrendered her pride because her passion was as great as his own.

This was the very thing she'd feared with Tony—this giving of herself, becoming his emotional slave. Yet that was exactly what she'd done with Chase. He ruled her head and her heart, as completely as Tony once had.

Fresh tears slipped down the side of her face, marking a slick trail, and she sniffled. Tucking her arms around her waist, she wondered how she would ever manage to fill up the time without Chase.

Chase impatiently filled out the registration forms at the Fairbanks hotel. The sooner he finished, the sooner he could call Lesley.

He wanted to kick himself. He'd known from the moment he arrived home that something was troubling her. He'd seen it in her eyes and in the way she preoccupied herself with making him something to eat. He should have settled matters between them right then.

Instead he'd selfishly satisfied his own physical needs, placing his demands above hers. Hell, he didn't know what was the matter with him. Lesley was like an infection that had gotten into his blood. But he wasn't interested in the anecdote. He lusted after his wife. There wasn't any other way to say it.

Once he had the key to his room, he paused and glanced longingly toward the coffee shop. He hadn't eaten since breakfast and that had been a quick cup of coffee and a blueberry muffin. Lunch had been prepared for him, but he'd opted to satisfy his carnal appetite rather than his physical one.

He'd eat later he decided, after he spoke to Lesley, after he explained, if that were possible. He couldn't lose her; she meant too much to him.

He let himself into the stark hotel room and after dumping his overnight bag on the bed, he sat on the edge of it and reached for the phone. His hand was eager as he punched out the number.

She answered on the second ring.

"Lesley, hello." Now that he could talk to her, he didn't know what to say. The need to explain himself had burned like acid the entire flight into Fairbanks, and now he was speechless.

"Chase?"

"I just arrived."

"Did you have a good flight?"

"I suppose. How are you?" He needed to know that before he proceeded.

"Fine."

Just the way she said it told him she wasn't. "I know it's probably not a good idea to have this conversation over the phone."

"We'll talk later," she said, and Chase feared that might be too late.

"I didn't want this misunderstanding to ruin what we have."

"And what exactly do we have, Chase?" she asked, her voice dipping to a mere whisper.

"A marriage," he returned without hesitation. "A fledgling marriage, which means we need to learn to communicate with one another. I'm going to need help."

"We'll learn," she said, but somehow that sounded forced, as if she wasn't sure they were capable of it.

"I'm sorry I didn't tell you more about Twin Creeks. There always seemed to be other things to discuss and it didn't seem all that important."

Lesley had no comment.

Chase pressed his hand to his forehead. "That isn't true," he said in a voice so low, he wondered if she heard him. "I was afraid that if you did know you'd change your mind about marrying me." He was taking one of the biggest risks of his life admitting that, but that was what made honesty of such high value. It was often expensive. But Lesley deserved nothing less than the truth.

"There'll never be a teaching position for me, will there?"

"No." Once more the truth stabbed at him with a wickedly sharp point.

"What did you expect me to do with my time?"

"Whatever you wanted. You can take correspondence courses, teach them if you want. Sometime you might want to start a business. Whatever you choose will have my full emotional and monetary support. I didn't bring you to Alaska to be my personal slave. Beyond anything else, I want you to be happy."

"In theory that all sounds well and good, but I don't know how it'll work in practice."

"Time will prove otherwise." He felt as though he were fighting for the heart of his marriage. Either he convinced her here and now that he was serious or he would lose her. Not now but sometime later, sometime down the road.

He couldn't bear to think of his life without her now. It seemed impossible that she could own such a large part of his heart after so short a time. "Give us a chance—that's all I'm asking."

"All right," she agreed in a deep whisper.

Chase scowled into the receiver. He didn't know if what he'd said had made a difference with her or not.

Chase had told her there was beauty in every part of Alaska but some of it wasn't immediately obvious. The beauty around Twin Creeks was dark with a splintered feel and look. Lesley stood outside the four-wheel-drive vehicle. She couldn't shake the feeling that life was very fragile in this part of the world.

The colors she saw thrilled her. Wild splashes of vibrant orange, purple and red painted the grassy and lichened meadows. Pencil-thin waterfalls delicately traced vertical slopes, pooling into a clear lake. The valley was lush, not like the rain forest of western Washington, but filled with life.

A moose grazed in the distance and she wondered if the great beast was plagued by mosquitoes the same way she'd been. Pete hadn't been teasing. These were the most irritating and the most persistent variety she'd ever encountered.

She'd found the keys to Chase's truck in a kitchen drawer. After less than twenty-four hours on her own, she was going stir-crazy. Chase had been adamant about her not exploring on her own, but she didn't have much choice. If she had to stay inside the cabin one more minute, Lesley was convinced she would go mad.

It was time she introduced herself to the ladies of Twin Creeks, she decided, but she'd gotten sidetracked on her way into town.

The sight of the moose in the meadow had captured her attention and she'd pulled off to the side of the road to watch.

She'd soon become engrossed in the landscape. With time on her hands, she lingered, enjoying the beauty but appreciating the dangers. After a while, she climbed back inside the truck and drove toward town.

Twin Creeks itself wasn't even a wide spot in the road. She'd visited rest stops that were bigger than this town. She counted three buildings, a grocery store and combination gas station, tavern and tiny post office. There wasn't even a church!

The sidewalks, if she could call them that, were made of wood that linked the three main structures. A handful of houses spotted the distance.

Lesley parked and turned off the engine. A face peered out from behind the tattered curtains in the tavern. She decided to pretend she didn't notice and got out of the car, walking toward the grocery. If she remembered correctly, Thelma Davis ran the store.

"Hello," Lesley said to the middle-aged woman behind the counter, determined to be friendly. "I'm Lesley Goodman, Chase's wife."

"Thelma Davis."

Lesley glanced around, pretending purpose had driven her into town instead of her own loneliness. Thelma must have a prospering business. She not only carried staples, but rented videos, sold yarn and other craft supplies, in addition to a variety of just about everything else.

"I heard this morning that Chase had married," Thelma said, coming around the counter. "Welcome to Twin Creeks. Everyone around these parts is fond of Chase and we hope you'll be real happy."

"Thank you."

"Ever been to Alaska before? Don't answer that. I can see by the look of you that you haven't. You'll never be colder in your life, that much I promise you. Some say this is really what hell will be like. Personally, I don't intend on finding out."

"How long have you lived here?" Lesley wanted to know.

Thelma squinted as she calculated the years. "We were one of the first ones to move up this way when word came that the pipeline was going through. That's been more than twenty years now. We love it, but the winters take some getting used to."

That Lesley could believe.

"We'll want to have a party for you two. I hope you don't mind us throwing a get-together in your honor. It's about all we can do for entertainment here, but we do our best to have fun."

"I love parties."

Thelma's hands rested against her hips as she sorted through her thoughts. "We'll have it at our home since we've got the biggest living room in town. Are you and Chase thinking of starting a family soon? It's been several years now since we had a baby born in Twin Creeks."

"Ah . . ." Lesley wasn't sure how to answer that.

"Forgive me, Lesley, it's much too soon to be pressuring you about babies. It's just that we're so happy to have another woman, especially a young one."

"I'm pleased to meet you, too."

"If you have a minute I'll call Margaret and get Heather and we can have coffee and talk. Do you have the time for that? Everyone is dying to meet you, even Gladys. We're eager to do whatever we can to help you feel welcome."

"I'd love to meet everyone." The sooner the better. If Chase was going to be away often, her link with the others would be vital to her sanity.

"I knew I was going to like you." Thelma grinned. "The minute Pete mentioned Chase had brought back a wife and described you, I knew then we'd be good friends. I think Pete's half smitten with you himself, which to my way of thinking, is good. It's about time the men in this community thought about settling down and starting families. That's what Twin Creeks really needs."

Lesley couldn't agree more.

She stayed and met the other women in Twin Creeks and by the time they finished they'd talked for two hours or more. Rarely had Lesley been more impressed with anyone. They were like the frontier women of old: resourceful, independent, with a well-developed sense of community. After the first half hour with the four others, Lesley felt as if she'd known them all her life. The genuine warmth of her welcome was exactly what she needed. When she returned to the house, she felt excited to be a part of this small, but thriving community.

Lesley wasn't home more than five minutes when the phone rang. She answered it eagerly, thinking it would be Chase. There was so much she wanted to tell him.

"Hello."

"Lesley, it's your mother." Their conversations invariably started with June Campbell-Sterne announcing her parental status as if Lesley had forgotten.

"Mom?" She couldn't have been more shocked if Daisy had arrived on her doorstep.

"It's true then, isn't it? You're married and living with some crazy man in Alaska."

"Mom, it isn't as bad as it sounds."

"When Tony contacted us—"

"Tony?" Lesley said, fuming. Daisy had warned her that her former fiancé was up to no good, but she never dreamed he'd resort to contacting her family to make trouble.

"Tony had the common decency to contact us and let us know you'd married, which is more than I can say for you."

"Trust me, Mom, Tony didn't have my best interests at heart."

"I don't believe that."

"He's being jealous and spiteful."

Her mother breathed in deeply as if she needed to control her temper. "All I want to know is if it's true you married a man who advertised for a wife on a Seattle billboard."

"Mom . . ."

"It is true?"

"Yes, but I didn't answer his advertisement, if that's what you're thinking. I know you're hurt," she said, trying to diffuse her mother's disappointment and anger, "and I apologize for not letting you know, but Chase only had a couple of days left in Seattle and you and Ken were traveling."

"As it happened, we returned early, but you didn't know that because you just assumed we were gone. You're my only child. Didn't you stop to think that I'd want to be at your wedding?"

"Mom, I'm sorry."

"Tony claims you don't know the man you married. That you weren't even in your right mind. He sounded very worried about you."

"None of that's true. I'm very happy with Chase."

"I won't believe that until I see you for myself and meet this man you've married. Ken's already made the flight arrangements for me. I'll be leaving first thing tomorrow morning and landing in Fairbanks at some horrible hour. I have no idea of how to reach Twin Creeks from there, but I'll manage if I have to go by dogsled."

"I'll fly down and meet you in Fairbanks," Lesley suggested, thinking quickly. "Then we'll fly back together." She was anxious for Chase to meet her mother, but she would have rather waited until they'd settled into their lives together.

"All right." Some of the defensiveness in her mother's voice was gone.

"If you want to talk to anyone about me and Chase, I suggest you contact Daisy instead of Tony."

"It broke my heart when you broke your engagement to Tony," her mother continued.

"Mother, he married someone else. I didn't break the engagement—he did...despite the claims he's making now."

"Look what's happened to you. Just look."

"Mother, I'm married to a wonderful man."

"I'll judge that for myself. I'll see you tomorrow." She listed her flight time and schedule and Lesley wrote it down on a yellow pad by the phone. Now all she needed to do was find the means of reaching Fairbanks and meeting her mother's plane.

"What do you mean she isn't at the house?" Chase demanded of his friend. He'd spent the most frustrating day of his life, first having to deal with the motor company and then attempting to contact Lesley. He'd tried earlier that afternoon and there wasn't any answer.

There were any number of reasons why she hadn't answered the phone, but when he tried fifteen minutes later and she was gone, he'd started to worry. Two hours of no response and he was beside himself. He called Pete and had his friend drive out and check out the cabin for himself.

"The door was locked," Pete explained, "so I couldn't get inside. What did she lock it for?"

"Lesley's from the city—they lock everything there," Chase explained, trying to think where she might possibly have gone.

"When she heard how small Twin Creeks was, she seemed upset," Pete said, sounding guilty and unsure.

"We already settled that," Chase insisted, growing irritated with his best friend. "Where the hell could she be?" The possibilities of her encountering danger fell like dominoes across his mind. "Do you think she might have wandered away from the cabin?"

"No."

Chase stiffened. "What makes you so certain?"

"The car's gone."

"The car. For the love of heaven, why didn't you say so sooner?"

He felt Pete's hesitation from a distance of several hundred miles. "There's something you're not telling me."

"Chase, damn it, you're my best friend. I don't want to be the one to tell you your wife walked out on you."

"Lesley's left?" The constriction in his chest was powerful enough to produce a sharp pain. "She drove?" His heart did a wild tumble as he mentally calculated how long it would take him to rent a car and catch her.

"No," Pete explained, "she drove out to the field and left the car there. She paid Jim Perkins to fly her into Fairbanks."

"I see." The hell if he did. "Without a word to anyone, she just up and left?"

"I'm sorry, Chase, I really am."

"What time will she be landing?"

"I can't be certain. All I know is what I heard from Jim at the field, and he told me everything he knew. He only heard part of the conversation. What are you going to do?"

"I don't know yet." Chase was in shock. His wife of less than a week had deserted him.

"You aren't going to let her go, are you?"

"No." He'd find Lesley, somehow, someway, and convince her to give their marriage a chance.

Chapter Twelve

"Mom." Lesley stepped forward and hugged her mother as June Campbell-Sterne stepped out of the jetway. Unexpected tears sprang to Lesley's eyes and she blinked them back, surprised by the ready display of emotion.

The tears were probably due to the restless night she'd spent in the hotel close to the airport. Apparently Chase hadn't returned to Twin Creeks the way he assumed, otherwise he would have read her message or answered her calls. He must be someplace here in Fairbanks. Unfortunately Lesley hadn't thought to get the name of his hotel since he'd originally planned to be in town only one night.

It seemed a bit ridiculous to contact every hotel in town and ask for Chase. The way things looked she'd be back in Twin Creeks before her husband.

"Let me get a good look at you," June insisted, stepping back while holding on to Lesley's shoulders. Her mother had tears in her eyes, as well. "Oh, sweetie, how are you?"

"I feel wonderful. See! Married life agrees with me." She wrapped her arm around her mother's waist and together they strolled toward the area where they could collect her luggage.

"I'll admit to being curious about your husband. Honestly, Lesley, what kind of man advertises for a wife?"

Lesley laughed, remembering that her own response had been similar. "He's not crazy—just resourceful. Honestly."

"I don't mind telling you, this whole matter of your marriage has both Ken and me concerned. It just isn't like you to marry a virtual stranger and take off to the ends of the earth."

"It isn't as bad as it seems."

Her mother sighed expressively. She was exhausted, as Lesley could well understand. "When will I meet Chase?" was June's next question.

Lesley wasn't entirely sure what to say. "Soon," she promised. "Listen, I've gotten us a hotel room. You're going to need to catch your breath before we fly back to Twin Creeks."

"I don't mind telling you, this was the longest flight of my life. I swear Antarctica would have been closer. For the life of me, I can't see you living in Alaska and liking it. You've lived in a big city all your life."

"You love Montana, don't you?"

"Yes, but that's entirely different. Ken and I are retired."

"It isn't different at all. I've only been in Alaska a short while and I love it already."

Her mother pinched her lips together as if to keep from saying something argumentative. "If it's all the same to you, Lesley, I'd prefer to push on. I'll rest once we reach your home and meet this man you've married. Then and only then will I truly relax."

That posed something of a problem. "We can't, Mom."

"Can't do what? Meet Chase? I wondered why he wasn't here to greet me. One would think he'd be eager to meet your family. I don't imagine you've met his, either, have you?"

"Mom," Lesley said impatiently. It troubled her the way her mother was so willing to find fault with Chase and her marriage. No doubt that was Tony's doing. Even now, he continued to haunt her life, reminding her in the most blatant way that he was a poor loser. More and more she'd come to realize that Tony had never really loved her. Even more enlightening was the realization she no longer loved him. She couldn't feel as strongly as she did for Chase and love Tony. She missed Chase dreadfully.

"What?" June snapped.

"Stop trying to make Chase into some fiend. He's not."

"I notice he sent you to the airport by yourself," she said, in that superior way that had driven Lesley to the brink of hysteria as a teenager.

"Mother, Chase has a job. He was away on business when you called."

"I will be meeting him later then?"

"Of course." Lesley just wasn't sure exactly when.

They stood for several minutes at the luggage carousel until June collected her one large suitcase and her cosmetic case. Lesley took the larger of the two bags and carried it outside for a taxi.

By the time they arrived back at the hotel room, Lesley was pleased that Jim wasn't scheduled to collect them until early the following morning. It was apparent her mother was worn-out.

"Would you like me to order you something to eat?" Lesley asked.

"No, thanks." June shook her head and politely covered her mouth for a loud yawn. "If you don't mind, I'll lie back and close my eyes for just a moment."

"Of course I don't mind. Relax, Mom." Her mother curled up on top of the mattress and was softly snoring seconds later. Lesley silently slipped a sweater over her mother's shoulders and tiptoed to the other side of the room. Her intention was to read until her mother woke, but she must have fallen asleep, as well, because the next thing she heard was the sound of running water.

Lesley stirred, opened her eyes and realized her mother was showering. With June occupied, Lesley reached for the phone and dialed Chase. Again there was no answer and, discouraged, she gently replaced the receiver. Where could he possible be?

"What exactly did she say?" Chase demanded of Jim Perkins. It frustrated him to have this conversation by phone. It would have been easier to read Jim in person instead of being left to translate his slow, easy drawl over the phone. Jim had never been one to reveal much with either words or actions. If Chase could have talked to Jim in person, it might have helped to persuade him of the urgency of all this.

Jim took his own sweet time answering. "She really didn't have much of anything to say."

Jim was in his early forties and possessed a calm, relaxed attitude that had never troubled Chase until now, when he was desperate to learn everything he could about Lesley's departure from Twin Creeks.

"Surely you chatted during the flight."

"She's the congenial sort. Personally I didn't think much of this scheme of yours of advertising for a wife, but I was wrong. Half the men are talking about doing something like that themselves, seeing the kind of woman you brought back with you. I don't suppose it would work with me, though."

"What did you and Lesley talk about?" Chase asked, dragging the subject back to his disappearing wife.

"Nothing much," Jim said, again after a lengthy pause. "Mostly she asked about you."

"What about me?"

He seemed to need time to consider the question. "Nothin' in particular. Just how long you've lived in Twin Creeks and that sort of thing."

"Did she mention she was staying in a hotel?"

"She might have said something, and then again, she might not have, either. I don't recall her saying she was, now that I think about it."

It was difficult for Chase not to let his distress bleed into the conversation. It was bad enough Lesley had left him so soon following her arrival in Twin Creeks. But he wasn't ready to announce to the entire community that his bride of one week had deserted him. If that were true, it would come out soon enough.

"I appreciate your help, Jim. Thanks."

"I don't think you need worry about her," Jim added in that flat, lethargic drawl of his. "Lesley's got a good head on her shoulders. She can take care of herself."

"Yes, I know." That, however, didn't ease Chase's mind in the least.

No sooner had he finished with the call, when the phone rang. Chase grabbed hold of the receiver so fast, he nearly jerked the telephone off the end table. "Yes?" he snapped.

"It's Pete."

"What'd you find out?"

"Lesley's staying at the Gold Creek Hotel by the airport," came Pete's automatic reply. "Room 204."

"How'd you learn that?" Sometimes it was better not to know where Pete got his information, but Chase couldn't help being curious.

"I have my sources. And listen, she may be having second thoughts because she hasn't purchased an airline ticket yet. Or if she has, she's using an alias."

"You're sure about that?"

"Positive." Pete didn't leave room for doubt in his voice. "Did you get any sleep last night?"

Chase closed his burning eyes. "None."

"That's what I thought. You know, Chase, if she insists on leaving you can't make her stay."

This had been the source of an ongoing internal debate. He didn't want to lose Lesley, but he couldn't hold her prisoner, either. If she'd decided she wanted out of his life and out of their marriage then he couldn't stop her. Even if it meant she'd decided to return to Seattle and that bastard Tony. But by heaven he was determined to have his say before he let her run out on him.

"What are you going to do?" Pete asked.

"I don't know yet. I'll probably go to the hotel and see if I can talk some sense into her."

"That sounds like a good idea to me. I suppose you want to do this on your own, but if you'd like I'll come along for moral support and wait outside."

"No, thanks, but I appreciate the thought."

"No problem. That's what friends are for." Pete hesitated as if there was something else he wanted to say, but wasn't sure if he should.

"There's more?"

"Yeah." Again Pete hesitated. "I don't make it a practice of offering advice, especially when it comes to dealing with a woman. My history with the opposite sex leaves a lot to be desired."

"Just say what's on your mind." Chase didn't generally seek out wisdom; he lived and learned by his own mistakes. This was different, and he was worried. He'd assumed everything was peachy between them and was at a loss to explain what'd happened. He'd believed, foolishly as it turned out, that everything was good between them. That he could be so blind to her feelings had come as a shock.

"I wish now that I'd gone after Pamela," Pete admitted, and to the best of Chase's memory, it was the first time his friend had verbalized his feelings. "I've wondered a hundred times over what would have happened if I'd taken the time and the trouble to let her know how much I loved her, how much I needed her. If I had, she might have stayed and I wouldn't be living day to day regretting that I didn't do everything within my power to convince her I cared. Don't make the same mistake."

"I don't plan on it."

"Good." Pete paused once more, which was unusual. Chase's friend generally spoke his mind without forethought. "You love Lesley, don't you?"

Chase wasn't sure how to answer. He'd made love to her more times than he could count. The physical desire they shared for each other had taken them both by storm. He'd never had a time with a woman the way he had Lesley.

Marriage, when he'd first considered finding himself a wife, had been for convenience sake, to ease his loneliness. He was searching for a companion, a helpmate. A woman to share his company during the long, dark winter months. He wanted a wife so he could bond with another human being. Since his parents' deaths, he'd felt detached and isolated from life.

Love had never entered into the equation.

In time, he assumed it would be natural for the two of them to fall in love. You couldn't live with a woman day in and day out and not feel something for her.

This had been the error of his thinking, Chase realized with a start. In making love to Lesley, he'd thought to ease his body's carnal needs. In the past he'd made love for the mutual satisfaction afforded him. He was a generous lover, or so he'd been told. But he gave little of his inner self; his contribution was to the physical act they'd shared.

Chase hadn't expected marriage to change that. Making love was making love, and generally it was damn good. His one wish was that marriage wouldn't detract from that.

This, too, was an area where he'd erred. Marriage to Lesley had altered everything. Every time they made love, he offered her a little more of his heart. A little more of his soul. A little more of himself. Lovemaking had become more than a physical mating, it had taken on a spiritual bonding. Somehow, exactly when, he couldn't be sure, their hearts and souls had merged into one.

He thought about Lesley in bed waiting for him. She was so incredibly lovely, with her hair spilling out over the pillow. The mere memory of her was enough to tighten his loins, even now. His mind filled with the image of her smiling up at him and holding open her arms.

It felt like a knife in his belly to think that Lesley would walk out on him without so much as a word.

"You're right," Chase admitted after several profound heartbeats. "I do love her."

"Then do whatever you have to do to keep her," Pete advised sagely. "Even if it means leaving Twin Creeks. You can always find another job, but you may never find another Lesley."

His friend was right and Chase knew it. Now all he had to do was come up with a way of convincing Lesley to give their lives together a fighting chance.

He showered and changed clothes, flipped through the Fairbanks telephone directory for the address of the Gold Creek Hotel and ordered a cab.

It would have been better if he'd been able to give some thought to what he wanted to say, but he dared not delay a confrontation for fear he'd miss her completely.

Chase was grateful to Pete in more ways than one. His friend had insisted he could find Lesley through a variety of connections faster than he'd be able to do it. Chase hadn't been keen on sitting back and letting someone else do the footwork, but in the end it had proven beneficial. Pete had located her within twelve hours.

The taxi let him off in front of the hotel. His heart was beating like a tin drum in his ear. Even now he didn't know what he intended on saying.

That, however, didn't stop him from pounding against the hotel door of room 204. When she didn't immediately answer, he knocked again, harder this time, so loudly that the lady across the hall stuck out her head to see what was causing such a commotion. She tossed him an irritated look and returned to her room.

The door opened and Lesley stood before him. Suitcases sat like unanswered accusations in the background. Suddenly he was angry. He thought of Lesley as decent and honorable, certainly not the kind of woman who would walk out on her husband without thought.

"What the hell do you think you're doing?" he demanded, pushing his way into the room. Lesley was so startled that she stumbled two steps back before regaining her balance.

"Chase?" She closed the door and leaned against it as if needing its support. Her eyes were wide and round. The perfume she wore, roses, he guessed, or some such flower, came toward him like a warm welcome. It demanded all the strength of will he possessed not to haul her into his arms and beg her not to leave him. Chase, however, had too much pride for that.

"I don't understand," she said, looking up at him, her eyes so damned innocent that the struggle not to kiss her drained his strength.

"I may have made a few mistakes along the way, but I would have thought you'd have the common decency to talk matters out instead of running out on me."

"Running out on you? I just flew down to Fairbanks."

"Without so much as a word to me," he reminded her in clipped tones.

"I left you a note." Her voice was raised and agitated now, as well. She elevated her hands to rest against her hips and glared at him, fire leaping into her eyes.

"A note," he said as though he thought that humorous. "What the hell good does that do when I'm here in Fairbanks?"

Lesley knotted her hands into tight fists. "You didn't give me the name of the hotel where you were staying. How was I supposed to contact you?"

"So now it's my fault." Chase knew why he was arguing with her, because if he didn't, he was going to reach for her and kiss her senseless. Fifteen seconds after that, he'd have her on that bed, flat on her back. Revealing his weakness was not the position he intended to take in this matter.

"Yes, it's your fault," she cried.

"Lesley, who is this man?"

The voice came at him like a high fly ball straight out of the blinding afternoon sun. Chase whirled around to find an older woman dressed in a bright red housecoat with matching red slippers. Her hair was wrapped in a towel twisted into a turban.

"Mother..." Lesley sounded as though she was about to burst into tears. She gestured weakly toward him, before her hand fell lifelessly to her side. "This is Chase Goodman, my husband."

The woman glared at him as if he were the devil incarnate, as if he were living proof of every dreaded suspicion she'd harbored. "What's the matter with you, young man?"

"Mrs. Campbell-Sterne..."

"How dare you talk to Lesley this way! Have you no manners?"

Chase gave an excellent imitation of a salmon, his mouth opening and closing several times without so much as a word fragment escaping. He looked to Lesley, desperate for her to explain, but she'd turned her back to him and it seemed as if she were struggling not to weep.

"I'm sorry," he whispered, looking to his wife.

"As well you should be, young man. I don't mind telling you, I had my concerns about the kind of man Lesley had married. Now I can see that—"

"Would you mind if I spoke to my wife alone for a moment?" Chase interrupted. Lesley's arms were cradling her middle and she was staring out the window. She gave no indication that she'd heard him.

"I . . . I don't know what to say." Mrs. Campbell-Sterne's face filled with color and she appeared quite flustered. "I suppose I should dress."

"Thank you," Chase said. He waited until his mother-in-law had moved into the bathroom and closed the door before he approached Lesley.

He stepped behind his wife and went to rest his hands on her shoulders, stopping just an inch short. He waited a moment, briefly closed his eyes and then dropped his hands to his sides.

"I just made a world-class ass of myself, didn't I?"

Lesley nodded.

"You left me a note at the house explaining?"

Once more she answered him with an abrupt nod.

"What did the note say?"

"That my mother had phoned and was worried about me and our sudden marriage. She was terribly hurt that I'd gone through with the ceremony without contacting her. She insisted upon flying up immediately to meet you."

"The note said all that?" He didn't know what craziness had possessed him to think she'd walk out on him without leaving behind something that would tell him where she was. He could have saved them both a lot of grief if he'd given the matter any thought.

"Tony contacted Mom and Ken," Lesley went on to explain. "He claimed I'd married on the rebound and that I'd made a terrible mistake. He was hoping to undermine our relationship." Just the way Lesley said it, led Chase to believe Tony had succeeded.

Chase couldn't blame Lesley for believing that it might be true after the stunt he'd just pulled. Apologizing seemed grossly inadequate.

"You flew down to meet your mother." He wanted to kick himself for being so stupid. No doubt her mother thought Lesley had married a madman and then he'd quickly gone about proving her right.

"What possessed you to charge in here like a bull moose?" Lesley demanded, turning to face him. She'd rallied enough to place her hands on her hips and glare at him with the indignation of a righteous woman unduly wronged. He wished he had a camera so he could capture her look. They could post it on church doors.

"I'm waiting for an answer," she reminded him, impatient now that she'd collected her composure.

The salmon imitation returned. "I...I thought you left me," he mumbled.

"You're not serious, are you?" Her eyes, which he'd always found so bright and beautiful, were filled with disdain now.

It sounded so weak an excuse. "I couldn't let you leave."

"Why not?" she demanded flippantly.

Now was the perfect opportunity to confess how much he loved her, how his heart wouldn't survive without her, but he couldn't make himself say the words, not with her looking at him as if he should be arrested.

"What else was I supposed to think?" he flared. "You up and left."

"You left, too, and didn't return when you claimed, but I didn't immediately leap to some outrageous conclusion."

"That's different," Chase argued, disliking the turn their conversation had taken. He didn't want to quarrel, not when he yearned to take her in his arms, bury his face in her neck and breathe in her womanly scent. Not when all he could think about was holding her again, kissing her and making love to her.

"Can I come out now?" June demanded from the bathroom doorway. She'd changed into blue-and-green-plaid slacks and a light sweater. She was nearly as tall as Lesley, with the same clear, dark, intelligent eyes. Like Lesley, her thoughts were easily read. Chase wasn't left to guessing what his mother-in-law was thinking. He hadn't impressed her, nor had he done anything to reassure her that Lesley had made a wise choice in marrying him.

The worst of it was that he couldn't blame her.

"It's all right, Mom. You can come out."

"You're sure?" She said it as though Lesley need only say the word and she'd contact the police and have Chase physically removed.

"I'm afraid I've made a mistake," Chase said, hoping he could explain what happened and at the same time ease her mind about his and Lesley's relationship.

"You can say that again," June returned crisply.

"Perhaps we could discuss this over lunch." Feeding them both sounded like an excellent plan and once they were relaxed then he'd be able to smooth matters over.

Lesley's mother didn't look the least bit sure she wanted to step outside the hotel room with him. She cast a guarded look in Lesley's direction. "What do you think, dear?"

"That'll be fine," Lesley agreed, reaching for a white sweater, neatly folded at the foot of the bed. Chase moved to help her put it on, then changed his mind. Now wasn't the time to be solicitous. Lesley wouldn't appreciate it.

Chase chose the hotel restaurant since taking the two anyplace else in town would require a taxi. The lunchtime conversation was stilted at best. June asked him several questions, but his attention was focused on his wife. June would ask him something and he'd answer, but his gaze didn't waver from Lesley's. He was looking for her to say or do something, anything to ease his conscience.

He'd blown it. The door had been left wide open for him to explain the reason he'd reacted like a madman. He'd been out of his wits, thinking he'd lost her.

Chase loved her. It didn't get any simpler than that. All he had to do was open his mouth and say it. Just how difficult could it be? Apparently more so than he realized because he let the opportunity slip past.

"How long do you plan to visit?" Chase asked June, thinking ahead. He supposed he shouldn't have been so obvious, but he was he counting down the minutes until he could be alone with Lesley already.

"Five days," June returned stiffly. She looked to Lesley as though to suggest purchasing another plane ticket south would be highly advisable.

"I was able to get the new motor this morning," Chase said to Lesley. "We can leave for Twin Creeks as soon as you're ready."

"Mother?"

"Anytime. I'm anxious to see your home, although heaven knows you haven't had much time to settle in, have you?"

"No." Lesley wearily eyed Chase.

"I'll leave you here and be back within the hour to collect you," he said, reaching for the lunch tab. "Perhaps you'd care to come with me," he suggested to Lesley. He tried to appear nonchalant about it, but his heart was in his throat like a young boy eager to please.

She took several moments to consider his request. "I don't think I should leave Mother," she said flatly.

Chase's shoulders fell. So this was the way it was going to be.

Lesley couldn't remember being more furious with anyone in her life. The man was a bloody fool. She'd agreed to marry Chase, agreed to leave the life she'd made for herself, her friends, her career and nearly all her personal possessions, and he still didn't trust her. He assumed she'd walk out on him the minute his back was turned. That was what hurt so much. His complete lack of faith in her.

That he'd made her sound like the biggest liar to ever roam the face of the earth hadn't helped matters any. Lesley had spent the better part of the morning listing Chase's many fine qualities. By the time she'd finished she'd made it sound like her husband should be canonized.

Fat chance of that happening after the way he'd barged into their hotel room like King Kong run amok. He couldn't have come off in a worse light had he tried.

After Chase left, her mother went strangely silent. They sat on the end of the bed, staring straight ahead. The quiet seemed obtrusive but each time Lesley thought of something to say, she changed her mind. Her mother would see through her efforts to make small talk in a heartbeat.

"He isn't always like this," she said to fill the void.

"I certainly hope not."

"Chase is honest and hardworking."

"That remains to be seen, doesn't it?" her mother asked stiffly.

"You don't like him, do you?"

June paused. "I don't have much reason to, do I? I fear you've been blinded, Lesley. How can you possibly love this man? You don't really know him... You couldn't. Tony said Chase had disguised the truth."

"You can't trust Tony."

"And why not? He had the decency to contact us when my own daughter hadn't thought to let me know she was marrying. Now that I've met your husband, I can appreciate Tony's concern."

"Mother..."

"Hear me out, please. I've bitten my tongue for the last hour, trying not to say what I should have earlier, and didn't. You have nothing in common with Chase. You might have convinced yourself you're happy now, and are intent on making this ridiculous marriage work, but it isn't necessary."

"Mom, please, don't." It hurt that her mother thought her marriage ridiculous. Lesley was angry all over again with Chase for having put her in this impossible situation of having to defend him.

"I have to speak my peace or I'll regret it the rest of my life. I made the same mistake with your father." Her voice faltered slightly. "I knew the marriage wasn't going to work, almost from the first, but I was too stubborn to admit it. At one point I convinced myself I was deeply in love with him. I worked hard at making the best of the situation, giving more and more of myself until there wasn't anything left of me to give.

"My life was a living nightmare. That was when he walked out. To see you repeat my mistakes would be the most tragic thing that could happen to me."

Lesley felt like she was going to break into tears. "It isn't like that with Chase and me."

"I don't believe that, not after talking to Tony and meeting Chase for myself. He isn't right for you. Anyone with a brain in their head can see that."

"Mom..."

"Are you pregnant?"

"I...I don't think so."

Her mother sighed as though relieved. "Come back to Montana with me," June pleaded. "If you want to start over, do it there. There's always a need for good teachers. Don't make the mistakes I did, Lesley. Leave Chase now—before it's too late—and come back with me."

Lesley was so intent on listening to her mother that she didn't hear the door open. She felt Chase's presence long before she heard his words. He was studying her without emotion, without revealing a hint of his thoughts.

"Well?" he said. "Make up your mind, Lesley. What do you want?"

Chapter Thirteen

Lesley's mother was staring at her, too, pleading with her to cut her losses now instead of waiting ten or more years down the road when she had a child or two.

"I...I thought we'd already decided to return to Twin Creeks."

June's shoulders sagged with dismay. Chase hurriedly reached for their suitcases, as though he expected Lesley to change her mind. That irritated her, too. Her mother looked as if she were about to erupt into tears and Chase was behaving like Attila the Hun.

The flight into Twin Creeks seemed to take twice as long as before. These weren't seven-minute silences, but seventy-minute ones. Chase flew the four-seater, concentrating as hard as if he were flying an F-14 attack jet under siege. Lesley made several attempts to carry the conversation, but it became painfully obvious that neither her mother nor Chase were interested in making small talk.

When they landed at the tiny airfield, Pete and Jim were there to greet them. Lesley didn't understand what was going on between Pete and her husband, but the minute Pete saw her, he grinned broadly and gave Chase the thumbs-up sign. Chase, however, didn't seem to share his friend's enthusiasm although she didn't have a clue what was happening between the two men.

"This is where you live?" June asked, scowling, staring at the barren tundra that surrounded the town. "Why it's...it's like stepping back a hundred years in time." The words were more accusation than comment. Lesley noticed Chase's jaw tense, but he didn't say anything, which was just as well. Lesley doubted that her mother would be receptive anyway.

When they arrived at the cabin, Lesley waited curiously for her mother's reaction. June asked several questions, nodding now and again as Chase told of his and Lesley's life in Twin Creeks. Lesley was pleased with his honest, but brief responses. She added what little information she could.

"The guest room is down the hall," Chase explained, leading the way into the house.

June paused in the living room, staring curiously at the fireplace and the bookshelves in much the same way Lesley had earlier. Before leaving, Lesley had added several minor female touches to the house. A homemade quilt that had been her grandmother's was draped across the back of the rocking chair. A picture of her mother and Ken rested atop the television and a small figurine of a harbor seal made of ash from the 1980 Mount Saint Helens volcanic eruption was propped against a Sue Grafton mystery in the built-in bookcase.

"This has a homey feel to it," June said grudgingly before following Chase down the narrow hallway.

Lesley bit her tongue and traipsed after her mother. Already she could see this was going to be the longest five days of her life.

Chase was forced to wait until after dinner before he had a chance to speak to Lesley's mother alone. While his wife was busy with the dinner dishes, Chase casually suggested a drive into town.

June hesitated, but it appeared she had things she wanted to say to him, as well, and she agreed with a shake of her head. It was all very polite, but Chase had the feeling Samurai warriors approached one another the same way.

Chase stepped into the kitchen. Under normal circumstances, he would have slipped his arms around Lesley's waist, moved his hands beneath her sweater and cupped her breasts. But these weren't normal conditions. He was afraid of touching her for fear of being charged with behaving uncircumspectly. He swore his mother-in-law had the eyes of an eagle and the temperament of a polar bear.

"Your mother and I are going for a drive," he said as casually as he could, hoping Lesley would drop it at that. He should have known better.

She hurriedly finished rinsing the pan she'd used to bake fluffy biscuits and reached for a hand towel. "I'll come with you."

"Don't be offended, but we'd both rather you didn't."

Lesley blinked and leaned against the back of the sink. "I don't know that talking to my mother when she's in this frame of mind is a good idea."

"We either clear the air here and now, or all three of us are going to spend a miserable five days."

"But, Chase..."

"Honey, listen." He paused and glanced over his shoulder. June had gone for a sweater, but would return any moment. "You and I need to talk, too. I'm sorry about starting off on the wrong foot with your mother. I promise I'll do my damnedest to make matters right. I owe you that much and a whole lot more."

Lesley lowered her gaze and nodded.

"I realize June's not the only one I offended," he said gruffly, walking toward her. If he didn't kiss her soon, he was going to go stark raving mad. Lesley must have felt the same way because she moved toward him, her steps as eager as his own. His heart reacted immediately, gladdened that she wanted to end the terrible tension between them.

He clasped his hands about her waist and caught her, dragging her into the shelter of his arms. The pleasure of her mouth was familiar and intense. Hot sensation assailed him at the taste of her; the warm, womanly feel of her was the purest form of torture. The scent of her perfume was like walking into a field of wildflowers. Her breasts were pressed to his chest and Chase swore they seared holes straight through him. He would have liked nothing more than to lift her into his arms and carry her to their bed.

Lesley must have felt the same way because she was moving her hips against him in small, undulating movements that were quickly driving him over the edge. He tried to still her with his hands, flattening his palms over her buttocks and pressing her against the hard evidence of his need.

"Hmm." The sound of June clearing her throat behind him was like a bucket of cold water being tossed over his head. He reluctantly released Lesley and stepped away from her.

"We won't be long," he said, as evenly as he could.

June was fussing with her sweater when he turned around, smoothing out the sleeves. Her back was straight with unspoken disapproval. She looked prim and proper and determined to save her daughter from his nasty clutches. Chase sighed inwardly and prayed for patience.

Lesley followed them out to the front porch and leaned against the support beam while Chase opened the passenger door and held out his hand to help June inside. His mother-in-law ignored him and hoisted herself into the front seat of the four-wheel-drive vehicle.

So that was the way it was to be.

Knowing what to expect, Chase tossed a look over his shoulder to Lesley and shrugged. He'd do his best but he wasn't a miracle worker. He couldn't force Lesley's mother to accept him as her son-in-law, nor could he demand she give her approval to their marriage.

He climbed into the seat beside her, and started the engine. "I don't know if Lesley had the chance to tell you, but Twin Creeks is a small town," he said, as he pulled onto the dirt and gravel roadway. "The population is around forty."

"Forty," June repeated slowly. "Did Lesley tell you she was born and raised in Seattle?"

"Yes."

"There were almost that many students in her kindergarten class. What makes you think a woman who's been around a large populated area will adjust to the harsh reality of this Alaskan town?"

Chase was ready for this one. "Lesley knew Twin Creeks wasn't a huge metropolis when she agreed to marry me." True, there were certain aspects he hadn't told her, but she'd had the general idea.

"You haven't answered my question," June reminded him primly, her hands neatly clenched on her lap.

"I'm hoping love will do that."

"Aren't you asking a good deal of a woman you've only known a few weeks?"

"Yes, but—"

"It seems to me," Lesley's mother interrupted, "that neither one of you have given the matter much thought. Lesley won't last a month in this primitive life-style."

Chase was fast losing his patience. "It seems you don't know your daughter as well as you think."

"I beg your pardon," she snapped. "You think I don't know what you did, don't you? You seduced my daughter, convinced her to marry you and then practically kidnapped her in order to get her to move north with you."

Chase pulled over to the side of the road. He couldn't concentrate on driving and hold on to his temper both at the same time. It was either park or steer right off the road.

"Lesley mentioned you'd spoken to Tony. Apparently you're echoing what he said. Unfortunately you and I don't know each other well enough to be good judges of the other's character. You see me as some psychopath who's tricked your daughter into marriage."

"You can't blame me for that, after you charged into our hotel room that way, acting like a lunatic."

Chase closed his eyes with mounting frustration. When he collected himself, he continued in a calm, clear voice. "Arguing isn't going to settle anything. You believe what you must and I'll do my best to stay out of your way." He started the engine, intent on turning the vehicle around and heading back to the house. He'd tried, but hadn't lasted five minutes with June hurling accusations at him like tomahawk blades.

"Listen here, young man..."

"The last person who called me 'young man' was my junior high teacher," Chase retorted. "I'm a long ways from junior high so I suggest you either call me by name or keep quiet."

Indignation swelled her chest like helium in a balloon and Chase wondered how it was possible to love Lesley and feel so negatively toward her mother. The woman was as personable as a block of salt.

"What you fail to understand," Chase said, after a lengthy pause, "is that we both share something in common."

"I sincerely doubt that."

"We both love Lesley."

"Yes, but—"

"There aren't any qualifiers as far as I can see," he interrupted. "She's your daughter, the woman you've raised and nurtured and loved all these years. I don't have the same history with her that you do, but I love her. Right now those may be only words to you, but I'd rather die than hurt her. If your main concern is that she won't adjust to life here in Alaska, then let me assure you, we'll move."

"This all sounds very convenient if you ask me. You're telling me what I want to hear."

"I'm telling you the truth." His anger flared briefly and then quickly died down. "We made a mistake in not contacting you about the wedding. If you're looking to blame someone for that, then I'll accept the guilt. I was in a hurry—"

"You rushed her into making a decision."

Another argument was poised and ready, but Chase recognized early on that there was nothing he could say that would alter Lesley's mother's opinion of him.

"I don't think we're going to be able to talk this out," he said, not bothering to disguise his disappointment. "I'd never keep Lesley here against her will, that much I promise you. You've raised a wonderful woman and I love her more than my own life. I can't offer you any more reassurance than that."

His words were greeted with silence.

"You and your husband will always be welcome here, especially after we decide to start our family."

She turned and glared at him as if he'd said something offensive, but Chase was tired of trying to decipher this woman's thoughts.

"If Lesley wants to visit you and your husband in Montana, she can go with my blessing," he added. It went without saying that he wouldn't be welcome. "I apologize for making an ass of myself earlier. I don't blame you for thinking ill of me, but I'd hoped we'd be able to put that behind us and start again. Perhaps before you leave, we'll be able to do that." He switched gears, turned the vehicle around and headed back to the house.

Lesley was knitting in the rocking chair when he walked into the front door. She glanced up anxiously, but must have read the defeat in his eyes, and the disdain in her mother's, because she sagged against the back of the rocker.

"What are you knitting?" June asked, revealing some enthusiasm for the first time in several hours.

"A sweater for Chase. One of the ladies in town sells yarn and so I picked up a pattern and everything else I was going to need while I was there."

"You met Thelma?" Chase asked, claiming the recliner next to his wife.

"I had tea with all the ladies," Lesley informed him. She was trying not to smile. The edges of her mouth quivered and the need to kiss him was nearly overwhelming.

So she'd gone into town on her own. Chase should have realized she was too anxious to meet the others to wait for him to introduce her around.

"It's stuffy in here," June announced.

"There's a chair on the porch," Chase suggested, eager to be with Lesley. If his curmudgeon of a mother-in-law wasn't standing guard over him, he might be able to steal a few minutes alone with his wife.

"I think I'll sit a spell out there."

"Good idea," Chase said with just a smidgen of glee. To his credit, he didn't lock the door behind her.

"What happened?" Lesley asked in a breathy whisper, the instant her mother was out the door.

"She thinks I seduced you into moving up here with me."

Lesley batted her long lashes at him. "You did, didn't you?"

"I'd certainly like the opportunity to do so again," he said, wiggling his thick brows suggestively. "I'm not going to last another five days without making love to you. Maybe not even another five minutes—"

"Chase!" Lesley whispered heatedly as he moved toward her. "My mother is right outside."

"She already thinks I'm a sex fiend as it is."

"You are!"

Chase chuckled, but his humor was cut short by a piercing scream from the front porch. Never in his life could Chase remember moving faster. Lesley reacted quickly, as well. Her knitting needles and a ball of yarn flew toward the ceiling as they each raced out the front door.

June was backed against the front of the house, her back flattened and her hands pressed over her heart. Even from this distance, Chase could see she was trembling.

"What happened?" Chase demanded.

June closed her eyes and shook her head. Luckily Lesley was there to comfort her. She wrapped her arms around her mother and gently guided her toward the front door.

"Something must have frightened her," Chase said. He debated about going for his hunting rifle, then decided against it. Whatever the danger had been, it'd passed.

"It was . . . huge." The words were strangled from June's throat.

"A bear, Mom. Did you see a bear?" Lesley's eyes clouded with fear at the thought.

"It must have been a moose," Chase speculated. He recalled the first time he'd come nose to nose with one. It was an experience he wasn't looking to repeat.

"No." June violently shook her head.

"A wolf?" Lesley pressed.

Once more his mother-in-law shook her head. Lesley led June into the house and set her down in the rocker while Chase went for a glass of water.

"It was a spider," June announced, gripping hold of the water glass with both hands. "A black one with long legs. I . . . I've never liked spiders."

Judging by June's reaction, that was a gross under-statement.

"A spider?" Chase whispered as Lesley left the room. The woman had sounded as though she'd barely escaped with her life.

His wife shrugged and rolled her eyes.

"Suggest she go to bed and rest," he offered next in hushed tones.

Lesley's lips quivered once more with the effort it took to suppress a smile.

Damn, but he wanted to smother her mouth with a kiss when she did that. From the gleam in Lesley's eyes, he knew she recognized his ulterior motives immediately. He hoped his wife shared his need because he was about to go crazy.

"Maybe you'd better lie down," Lesley suggested.

It was all Chase could do not to leap into the air and scream *yes*.

"You're right," June said, clearly shaken by the en-counter. "I don't generally overreact like this. It's just that this spider was so big. I didn't expect there to be spiders here in Alaska, of all places."

"We all have a tendency to overreact under certain circumstances," Chase said, using the opportunity to defend his own behavior earlier in the day. "Later we re-alize how foolish we must have looked to everyone else. People generally understand and forgive that sort of thing." As far as sermons went, he felt he'd done well. He was no television evangelist, but he got his point across. Hopefully, June picked up on his message.

"I do feel like I should rest."

"I'll check out the room," Chase offered, "and make sure there's nothing there." All he needed was for June to interrupt him and Lesley. He didn't know how well his heart would stand up to another bloodcurdling scream.

"Thank you," June whispered.

Lesley went with her mother into the bedroom. After five minutes Chase was glancing at his watch, wondering how long this was going to take.

Another ten minutes passed before Lesley returned to the living room. "Mother's resting comfortably. I gave her a couple of aspirin and hope that'll help settle her nerves."

"I need something to settle my nerves, too," Chase said, reaching for her and pulling her onto his lap.

"Chase." She put up a token struggle.

"Kiss me."

"I . . . I don't think that's such a good idea."

"Considering what I really want, a kiss seems damn little. Don't be stingy, honey, I need you." She hadn't a clue, which was just as well, of how badly. He couldn't hold her this intimately and not have his blood temperature rise. If they'd been alone, he'd have had her in his bed fifteen seconds after they reached the house. As it was, he'd been forced to sit through a stilted dinner and then deal with her dragon of a mother before and after the spider attack. A kiss was damn small compensation.

He nibbled at her ear, resisting the urge to take her breasts. That would have led to other delights and he was trying to keep matters under control. A kiss was all he wanted, just enough to satisfy him until he could tell her all that was in his heart.

He could feel what little resistance there was in Lesley melt away. She squirmed in his lap, tormenting him.

Lesley turned her head until their lips met. The kiss was slow and deep. By the time they finished, Chase swore there wasn't a part of his body that wasn't throbbing with need.

It demanded every shred of stamina he possessed to drag his mouth away from hers. By that time, Lesley's arms had circled his neck and she was sighing softly. She pressed her head to his shoulder and worked her fingers into his hair. She wanted him. He knew by the little whimpering sounds she made that came deep from her throat that she was as eager to make love as he was.

Now was the time to tell her. He forced his mind from the warm, rich feel of her body pressing against his, of her moist breath fanning his neck. Her breasts, nestled against his chest, were more temptation than any man should be forced to endure.

"When I spoke to your mother..." The words felt like lead weights against his lips. Maybe this would be easier after they made love.

"Yes?" Lesley lifted her head, curiosity brightening her eyes.

"I told her something I've never told you." Their eyes met and he wiped the moisture from her swollen lips with his thumb. Her thoroughly kissed mouth widened briefly with a smile. The tip of her tongue appeared to goad him into kissing her again. Chase knew if he did, any chance of telling her how much he loved her would be lost. Instead he'd be showing her in the most graphic of ways, with his body pumping into hers, and fire consuming them both.

"I love you, Lesley." There it was, out in the open for her to either accept or deny. His heart was there, too, along with his dreams for their future.

Lesley tensed, her hands were on his shoulders, her nails biting into his flesh. "What did you just say?" Her voice was barely audible as though she wasn't sure she'd heard him correctly.

"I love you." It sounded so naked saying it like that, without any qualifiers or additions. "I realize blurting it out this way makes you uncomfortable, but I didn't think it was fair for me to tell your mother how I felt about you and say nothing to you."

She was off his lap in a flash, as if sitting with him like that had suddenly burned her. Tears coated her eyes as she backed away from him.

"I realized it when I thought you'd deserted me," he explained. "I'd tried to reach you by phone and when I couldn't I had Pete come out to the cabin. He told me the truck was gone and that Jim had flown you into Fairbanks. I didn't know what to think. Now it seems ludicrous to leap to the conclusions I did, but at the time it all made perfect sense."

"I see." One tear escaped the corner of her eye and rolled down the side of her face. It might have been his imagination, but it seemed she'd gone pale.

"Say something," he pleaded. His heart was precariously perched at the end of his sleeve. The least she could do was let him know if it was about to topple.

"I knew when we married you didn't love me," she said, without looking at him. "I accepted that. When we were in Canada...I knew you didn't love me then, either."

"Don't be so sure," he returned, frowning. He knew the problem, had always known the problem. Tony. She was in love with her former fiancé and that wasn't likely to change for a good long while.

Her head snapped up. "You were in love with me on our honeymoon?"

He shrugged, unwilling to reveal everything quite so soon. It'd help matters tremendously if she expressed her feelings for him.

"Were you?" she pressed, louder.

Chase stood and rubbed his hand along the back side of his neck, walking away from her. "Does it matter?"

"Yes."

"All right," he muttered. It was apparent she was going for the jugular. "As near as I can figure I loved you when we married. It just took me awhile to put everything together." He stuffed his hands inside his pants pockets. This wasn't going nearly as well as he'd hoped.

"I tried to reassure your mother, but that didn't work out," he continued. "Tony's got her convinced you married me on the rebound and it was a mistake for us both."

"I didn't."

Now it was Chase's turn to go still. His heart was beating hard and fast. He was afraid to believe what he thought she was saying.

"You aren't in love with Tony?" he asked.

"That would be impossible when I'm so crazy in love with you." She smiled then, that soft womanly smile that never failed to stir him. To stir his heart and his loins. Her eyes were clear and bright and her love shone through like a beacon.

Chase closed his eyes to savor her words, to wrap them around his heart and hold on to the feeling. It happened then, a physical need, a craving for her that was so powerful it nearly doubled him over. He was instantly hard. Hard like he'd never been hard before. His need was like a frenzy, much too potent to control.

They moved toward each other, their kisses fuel to the flames of their desire, which was urgent and demanding.

"Chase," Lesley groaned between hard, moist kisses, unbuttoning his shirt as she spoke. "We can't.... Mother's room is directly down the hall from us. She'll hear."

Chase kissed her while trying to decide what to do, which proved to be a mistake. Much more of this and he would end up throwing caution to the wind and making love to her right in the middle of their living room.

"The cache," he said, thanking God for the inspiration. It wasn't the ideal solution up there with his stored goods, but it would serve their purposes.

Lesley's legs seemed to have given out on her and he lifted her into his arms, pausing only long enough to grab the bedspread from the bed and carry it outside with them.

Having Lesley climb the ladder ahead of him stretched the boundaries of his control to their limit. She was three steps ahead of him, with her rounded buttocks at eye level. The temptation was more than a mortal man should be asked to bear. Chase couldn't resist. He closed his eyes and followed her up the steps.

The area was dark, which suited Chase, and tightly packed. He pushed several boxes aside, spread the quilt onto the hard surface. Urgency dictated his movements. Once the blanket was in place, he stripped and reached for his wife.

The time for preliminaries was long past. Their need for one another was far too intense for anything but mating.

Lesley was on her back, her clothes as carelessly tossed aside as his own, lifting her slender arms to him.

He tried to speak, tell her how much he loved her, promise her the stars and moon, but when he opened his mouth, his words were gruff and shaking and he wasn't sure she could understand him.

He parted her legs with trembling hands; the skin of her inner thighs felt like silk against his callused hands. Holding his breath, he pushed forward and entered her warm, tight welcome.

Chase groaned.

Lesley sighed.

Neither moved. The pleasure was too keen to do anything but savor it.

Lesley recovered first, locking her legs around his waist. Then she arched her back, increasing the tension and the ecstasy. Chase had assumed that was impossible.

He must have moved, but he wasn't aware of the hard thrusts of his body. Only when Lesley cried out with her completion did he realize what had taken place. His own climax followed hers in a white-hot eruption that tossed his senses into oblivion. Only when the last spasms of pleasure faded did he breathe.

His hands were in her hair, hers in his, and they were kissing again. Chase tasted her tears. He hadn't meant for Lesley to weep, hadn't meant to be so damned crass as to take her without foreplay, but the need had been too great.

He gathered her in his arms, holding her close with a fierce possessiveness until their breathing became normal once again.

"I love you." Each time he said it, the words came easier.

"I know." She spread a slow series of kisses along the edge of his jaw.

"Your mother..."

"Don't you worry about Mom. She'll come around, especially when she's got a handful of grandchildren to spoil."

"Children," Chase said softly.

"Is this a new concept to you?"

"Not entirely. I fully intend on making you a mother."

"Good." Her teeth caught his lower lip and she brought it into his mouth, and sucked on it, using her tongue to entice him even further. "Soon I hope."

"How soon?" It seemed impossible that his body could be ready for her again, but the reality of his need was too blatant to ignore.

Lesley raised her head and her beautiful dark eyes smiled down on him. "There's no time like the present, is there?"

Chase sucked in his breath. He'd thought to wait a year, possibly longer, to start their family, but refusing Lesley anything was impossible, especially when she insisted on rotating her hips against him.

"Will I ever grow tired of you?" he wondered aloud.

"Never," she promised.

Chase grinned and instinctively knew it was true.

Epilogue

"Grandma, Grandma." Three-year-old Justin Goodman raced from Lesley's hold as they stepped out of the jetway and he ran into the waiting arms of June Campbell-Sterne.

June hugged her grandson to her breast and lifted him from the ground. "My, oh my, you've gotten so big."

Justin's chubby arms circled his grandmother's neck and he squeezed tightly.

"Justin's not the only one who's grown," Chase said, wrapping his arm around Lesley's thickened waist.

"You would be, too, if you were about to have a baby," Lesley reminded her husband.

Chase chuckled and shook hands with Ken Sterne.

"It's good to see you again," Ken said, grinning. "June's been cooking for three days. You'd think an army was about to descend upon us."

"Shush now," June chastised her husband. "How are you feeling?"

Lesley sighed. How did any woman feel two months before her delivery date? Anxious. Nervous. Eager. "I'm okay."

"It's good to see you," June said, kissing Chase on the cheek.

Chase's eyes met Lesley's and he gave her a know-it-all look. It had taken time, but the bridges had been mended. Lesley had been right about the effect grandchildren would have on the relationship between her mother and her husband. When they first met, four years earlier, her mother was convinced Chase was some kind of demon. These days he was much closer to sainthood.

"How's Twin Creeks?" Ken asked, steering the small party toward the area where they could collect their luggage.

"The population has doubled," Lesley informed him proudly. It had started soon after her arrival. Pete had gotten married the following spring and he and his wife already had two children and another on the way. Even Jim had married, which surprised them all. A widow with four children had made a place in all their hearts.

It seemed there was a baby being born every few months. The community was thriving. Lesley couldn't help believe Chase was the one who'd put the wheel into motion. His venture into Seattle to find himself a wife was what had started the process. Soon the other men working at the pump station were willing to open their lives.

Chase and Lesley had argued this point often. Chase was convinced once the other men saw what a wonderful woman he'd found, they'd decided to take their chances, as well.

Whatever the reason, there were fifteen more women residing in Twin Creeks. Ten childbearing women, who seemed to make it a personal goal to populate Alaska.

She looped her arm around her husband and smiled softly to herself. How different her life would have been without him. Each and every day she thanked God for that crazy advertisement she'd seen on her way to the store.

BRIDE WANTED.

She was even more grateful he'd chosen her, because this was the grandest adventure of her life.

*   *   *   *   *

Look for Marriage Wanted *by Debbie Macomber,*
the next book in FROM THIS DAY FORWARD.
Coming in October from Special Edition.

Silhouette SPECIAL EDITION

It takes a very special man to win *That* SPECIAL *Woman!*

She's friend, wife, mother—she's you! And beside each Special Woman stands a wonderfully special man. It's a celebration of our heroines—and the men who become part of their lives.

Look for these exciting titles from Silhouette Special Edition:

Don't miss THAT SPECIAL WOMAN! each month—from some of your special authors! Only from Silhouette Special Edition!

TSW3

Silhouette® SPECIAL EDITION®

WILD RIVER TRILOGY

by Laurie Paige

Come meet the wild McPherson men and see how these three sexy
bachelors are tamed!

In HOME FOR A WILD HEART (SE #828) you got to know
Kerrigan McPherson. Now meet the rest of the family:

A PLACE FOR EAGLES, September 1993—
Keegan McPherson gets the surprise of his life.

THE WAY OF A MAN, November 1993—
Paul McPherson finally meets his match.

Don't miss any of these exciting titles—only for our readers and only
from Silhouette Special Edition!

Silhouette
SPECIAL EDITION

From this day forward

**Coming in September,
the second book in an exciting trilogy by**

Debbie Macomber
BRIDE WANTED

Advertising for a bride on a billboard may have been brazen, but it got
Chase Goodman what he wanted—beautiful Lesley Campbell. And
now he wanted much more....

FROM THIS DAY FORWARD—Three couples marry first
and find love later in this heartwarming trilogy.

Look for
MARRIAGE WANTED (SE#842) in October.
Only from Silhouette Special Edition.

Silhouette Books has done it again!

Opening night in October has never been as exciting! Come watch as the curtain rises and romance flourishes when the stars of tomorrow make their debuts today!

Revel in Jodi O'Donnell's STILL SWEET ON HIM—
Silhouette Romance #969
...as Callie Farrell's renovation of the family homestead leads her straight into the arms of teenage crush Drew Barnett!

Tingle with Carol Devine's BEAUTY AND THE BEASTMASTER—
Silhouette Desire #816
...as legal eagle Amanda Tarkington is carried off by wrestler Bram Masterson!

Thrill to Elyn Day's A BED OF ROSES—
Silhouette Special Edition #846
...as Dana Whitaker's body and soul are healed by sexy physical therapist Michael Gordon!

Believe when Kylie Brant's McLAIN'S LAW —
Silhouette Intimate Moments #528
...takes you into detective Connor McLain's life as he falls for psychic—and suspect—Michele Easton!

Catch the classics of tomorrow—*premiering* today—
only from ▼ *Silhouette*

If you're looking for more titles by

DEBBIE MACOMBER,

don't miss these heartwarming stories by one of
Silhouette's most popular authors:

Silhouette Special Edition®

#09662	NAVY BRAT	$3.25	☐
#09683	NAVY WOMAN	$3.25	☐
#09697	NAVY BABY	$3.29	☐
#09744	STAND-IN WIFE +	$3.39	☐
#09756	BRIDE ON THE LOOSE +	$3.39	☐
#09798	HASTY WEDDING	$3.39	☐
#09831	GROOM WANTED*	$3.50	☐
	+ Those Manning Men		
	*From This Day Forward		

Silhouette® Books

#45152	BORROWED DREAMS	$3.59	☐
	(Men Made in America series—Alaska)		
#48254	TO MOTHER WITH LOVE '93	$4.99	☐
	(short-story collection also featuring Diana Palmer and Judith Duncan)		

TOTAL AMOUNT	$
POSTAGE & HANDLING	$
($1.00 for one book, 50¢ for each additional)	
APPLICABLE TAXES**	$ _____
TOTAL PAYABLE	$ _____
(check or money order—please do not send cash)	

To order, complete this form and send it, along with a check or money order for the total above,
payable to Silhouette Books, to: *In the U.S.:* 3010 Walden Avenue, P.O. Box 9077, Buffalo,
NY 14269-9077; *In Canada:* P.O. Box 636, Fort Erie, Ontario, L2A 5X3.

Name: _____

Address: _____ City: _____

State/Prov.: _____ Zip/Postal Code: _____

**New York residents remit applicable sales taxes.
 Canadian residents remit applicable GST and provincial taxes.   DMBACK2